Grab

Bag

3

FOR LITERARY HEAT

www.barbarianspy.com

This book is copyright © habu 2013
Published by BarbarianSpy in 2013
Cover design © S Bush 2013
Cover image: © Wrangel | Dreamstime.com
ISBN Print: 978-1-922187-25-3
All rights reserved

Published by BarbarianSpy
Jindalee St
Toronto, NSW 2283
AUSTRALIA

Grab Bag

3

by

habu

Table of Contents

Introduction

The third of habu's *Grab Bag* short story anthologies is much like the first two, a totally unthemed gay male story collection that skips over the world in location and across time in setting and offers a variety of thoughtful themes, romance, humor, hot sex, irony, twist and/or twisted endings, and much else that has dropped out of habu's fertile mind and into his computer on almost a daily basis during the past year. Included in this fifteen-story collection are, in addition to contemporary explorations of being an "actively gay male" in the United States, stories reflective of habu's past in Bangkok and Hong Kong; a few inspired by a recent trip to England, Wales, and Scotland, and even a short trip to Portugal as well as several exploring favorite themes of his: first times, older and younger men, black on white, surprise and unexpected twists, and the worlds of art and spies.

The anthology fittingly starts with a "first time" story, "The Awakening," of a young man doing just that—awakening to his sexuality and his preference as he's thrust out into the world from a protected childhood. From there, the anthology takes a wide turn to the humorous in "Best Job in the World," with a skin magazine editor receiving a surprise "thanks" visit from one of his unlikely authors. Turning to snarky, "Lance's Secret" is about the plight of a college fraternity house "reliever."

"Emmet" takes us to a university community, where a very proper university don develops a fixation on a black working-class neighbor and gives up all of his academic pretensions. "Ernestine," which continues the black and white element, is one of habu's rare explorations into the world of transvestites.

"Loving Wife" turns to a somber note, with a real-world look at the threat to an older-younger, same-sex marriage built on the sex drive when the older partner is dying from cancer.

We zip off next for Portugal in "Chaz's Choice" for a "rubber-meets-the-road" decision that has to be made in the nasty world of spying. "The Negotiator," the first of three England-based stories in the anthology, offers a different kind of espionage, as two men work each other as they each work to come out on top in an international business transaction.

"The Clothes Horse," takes us to Hong Kong for the story of a deal to exchange services for sexy men's clothes. In "The Video List," a young man in rural Virginia learns that it's more exciting and profitable to be in gay sex videos than to work in a video store. "The Celtic Sonata of Life" crosses the Atlantic to England's Cotswolds and a special service vacation cottage. "On a String in Bangkok" takes the reader back across the world for a habu reminiscence about gay life in Bangkok in the mid-seventies and the particular meaning of being "on a string."

In a change-of-pace and timing piece for this anthology, "Training Asu," set in an ancient Middle Eastern city, covers the coming-of-age initiation of a beautiful young man. "So You Want to Be in Movies" is the proverbial film producer office couch audition story, but laced with a bit of mystery and menace. The anthology ends with a historical piece set in Norwich, England, covering the developing professional life of a fine young artist who was willing to do anything to receive the mentoring of an older, accomplished artist.

The Awakening

I guess it may have been because of my mother—and of the strange beliefs my grandmother formed around her. Up until the time my grandmother's ill health coincided with me being old enough to go to college, I'd been kept in the dark about so many things. I knew that my mother must have done some really, really bad things from the way that my grandmother just tightened up, crossing her arms under her bust and screwing up her face and pursing her lips like she did any time that I asked about my mother. And let's not even talk about asking about my father. I learned early on that it wasn't a topic to bring up.

"Just go down the street and point out any man you see," Grandma would say in that tight voice of hers. And she'd be looking hard at Grandpa like he was just one more man on the street. He'd look away then, rustling that newspaper he was always reading, and mutter, "Let's just not go there, Marie. Remember your heart."

But my mother. I knew that they knew who my mother was, because she was their daughter. That was how I was their grandson. But they treated us like we were total opposites. And it was only recently that I realized that this was the goal: to make us total opposites. Any mention of my mother at all instantly brought tension into the room. She seemed always to be there, lurking somewhere, even though I didn't even know what she looked like. There was nothing in the house that physically could be associated with her. And the only time I asked Grandpa about her, he turned a stony face to me, peering from around the side of a newspaper page, and said. "Your mother is dead to us, son. We will not speak of that again."

Grandma, though, cleared that up. My mother wasn't really dead dead. She just was somewhere doing something that Grandma didn't want to talk about. And it was quite obvious that it was something I didn't need to know about—and certainly wouldn't be doing as long as I was in *her* house and with my feet under *her* table.

Other than that sore topic, though, my grandparents—well, mostly my grandmother—doted on me. Whereas nothing in the house spoke of my mother, at every turn there was a photograph of me: me seeing the Christmas tree for the first time; me on my first bicycle, with grandpa standing there, holding me upright and making me think I was doing that all by myself; Grandma putting a birthday cake in front of me. The weird thing about those photographs, though—and I only recently noticed that—was that the photographs were always just me—or me with either Grandma or Grandpa. There were no other people in my life. Not even any friends my own age. Maybe that's why later I gravitated to older men. I'd grown up with only old people around me.

That had been the way it was until I was ready to go off to college—which was only something that came to pass after a knock-down, drag-out fight between my grandparents, where Grandpa was saying that I couldn't be kept close all of my life and Grandma only seeing his point when she collapsed and Grandpa had to call in paramedics. When she was strong enough for them to talk again, Grandpa used her ailment to drive home his point, and Grandma just turned her face to the wall and didn't say another word.

Even then, though, I only went to the nearby junior college this past year. Up until then I'd been homeschooled.

I wasn't totally dumb about what my mother was doing that Grandma didn't like—or what growing up was all about. I'd done some experimenting, finding out all by myself what my body was about and how to gain pleasure from it. Of course I knew it was a forbidden pleasure—at least where my grandparents were concerned—and that it had something to do with my mother being a bad person. But it was only late in the summer that I realized that it wasn't just something I had invented—for myself—and then only because it gave me relief from some pent-up feelings.

This came about because of the slow awakening to the world that my grandfather was initiating. After getting Grandma to agree to letting me go on to college—and it wasn't because she wasn't doing a good job of schooling me, because I passed the entrance exams with flying colors even if it only was a community junior college—Grandpa also declared that I would have to help pay for the education, so I'd have to get a summer job. Where Grandma had been good about the textbook part of the schooling, Grandpa had been equally good at making sure that I grew up strong and trim. We had a basement gym room and he insisted that I follow an exercise and strength-training routine almost from the time I could walk. It was natural, then, that he set me up in a job where I would get good exercise.

He bought me two professional-level mowing machines—a big one for open stretches and a narrow one for trimming areas—and other equipment I would need to set up a lawn-mowing business. I started by offering to do work in the neighborhood and then branched out farther when I found that people were happy to pay someone else to mow their lawns while they went off to the gym.

What this is all leading up to, though, is Mr. Crabtree down the block—the football coach at the local high school I didn't get to go to. Now, he was certainly someone who could do his own lawn. He was always exercising and keeping his body toned and fit, and he was outside and on the field all summer getting guys ready to play football in the fall. So, mowing his own lawn would have been a lot cheaper than paying to go to a gym. But I guess he didn't see it that way.

I almost just bypassed his house when I was drumming up business, figuring he did his own lawn or, more likely, he got his football players to do it. But he jumped at my offer to do it. I mean really jumped at the idea. He was all smiles and glad handing and gushing about what a great idea it was and how in shape I looked and how he wondered how we could have been living in the same neighborhood all these years and never have come into contact.

* * * *

A lot of my customers this summer have been really friendly to me, but none more so than Mr. Crabtree. He always seems to be home when I come to mow, even though I know he is busy at school with summer practices. And he always insists that I come up on his back porch and have a cold drink and cool down after I've done the mowing. It's really been hot this summer, out there mowing. So hot that I was going through a lot of T-shirts, sweating, while I mowed. After the first couple of weeks Grandma complained about all of the extra washing she had to do and how stinky my work clothes were—so I began mowing shirtless. None of my customers complain, so I just keep on doing it.

Mr. Crabtree always has offered me a beer after I've mown, and I've always had to turn him down. I'm really not old enough in our town to be drinking beer and Grandma would have had a cow to hear that I drank anything alcoholic. Mr. Crabtree teases me about it, but he then goes back inside and comes out with a glass of lemonade or iced tea or Coke or something.

He's always done that: offered me the beer and then had to go back inside the house for something else for me to drink. The second time he did it was the first time I noticed that he had magazines sitting on the table next to the chair I sat on on the porch. When I first noticed them, I thought they had something to do with physical education—and thought it was natural that Mr. Crabtree would have magazines like that. But when I looked closer, I saw that they weren't like that at all. They had photographs of guys. And they didn't have a stitch on. Some of

12

the photos were of just one guy, but others were of guys like wrestling with each other or something.

The third time I mowed his lawn, I couldn't help it. I looked closer at those magazines. They weren't just wrestling.

Well, that set my mind going, I'll tell you. And it had an effect on parts of me other than my mind too. I found myself looking around to see if Mr. Crabtree was coming back and listening for signs that he was. He's been taking an ever-longer time getting my drinks, though, so it's giving me a chance to look at those magazines more closely. Last week I thought maybe he'd caught me looking at them. Out of the corner of my eye I thought I saw some movement in the window, in what I think is his dining room, out onto the porch, but when I turned to look there, I didn't see anything but what looked like the back of a dining room chair—and ruffling curtains.

After cutting his grass since then, though, I've been going home and going straight to the shower. Now while I shower, I think about those photographs I'm seeing in his magazines. And I'm taking care of myself. Since seeing those photographs, I've had more of that tension than ever before, and I look for relief. I wasn't taught shit about sex education, but I've discovered some things myself. And there's the Internet to help. And I've found that those photographs I saw on Mr. Crabtree's porch don't just come in magazines.

I know now what I'm doing, because I've looked it up. I'm masturbating, or, in more crude terms, jacking off. I didn't know anything about that sort of stuff before. It's nothing that my Grandma covered in her homeschooling and nothing that Grandpa has ever mentioned either. I haven't brought it up myself, because it's very clear to me that it's tied up in whatever badness my mother is doing—and any subject bordering on that sets my Grandma right off. I don't think her heart can take that sort of irritation anymore.

* * * *

Miss Rogers, my English teacher, has asked me to come to her office at school after class today. She asked me while I was standing there at the end of class with Tom Strong and Glen

Childress. This is the first day anyone has talked to me in class. I've gotten some friendly looks from some of the women, but this is the first time any of the men have said anything to me. The women seem to be older than me, mostly, but the guys are mostly like me—just out of high school and trying to work their way into college. They've been kind of standoffish, though, because I've been able to answer all of the questions that Miss Rogers answered—just like the women do—and I think the guys think I'm a show-off. Most of them didn't get very good grades in high school, I think. And I think that's why they're here instead of a better college. I'd like to work my way out of here and go to a better college.

I have to remember not to raise my hand in class when I know the answer to the question.

"You know what it means for Miss Rogers to ask you to her office after class, don't you?" Tom Strong asks with a smirk on his face.

"Means she's got the hots for you," Glen says. "Tom can tell you exactly what that means, can't you Tom?"

"She's old, but she's got as good a pussy as any of them do," Tom says, wagging his head. "Have fun, chum. Guess it pays off to answer her questions in class."

I'm not really sure what they mean as I go down the hall to Miss Roger's office. It's the last one down the hall of the teacher's rooms. The light is off in the room, and I almost don't go in. I almost just stand there at the end of the hall, waiting for her to show up.

"Is that you, Allen?" I hear her ask from inside her office. Her voice sounds a bit breathy. "Come on in and shut the door behind you."

As I enter her room, which isn't totally dark—she has a window and it's late afternoon—I notice that although her door has a glass window in it as they all do, hers is papered over from the inside.

She's sitting on her desk, one leg dangling in front of her and the other propped up on a chair pulled over to be right in front of the desk. Her skirt is pulled up over her knees, and I can see all the way up her plump thighs to hallelujah. She isn't

14

wearing any panties. There's a V of curly brown hair that I can see up there where her thighs meet.

I'm think that's strange—the color down there—because the hair on her head is blonde.

"It's great having someone in class this year who is ahead of the curve, Allen," she says in that breathy voice that is a lot different from what she has used in class this first week of the course. "You really are a grown man for your age. And I can't keep my eyes off of you. Anyone tell you how good you look? What a handsome young man you are? I'll bet you smell as good as you look. Come here closer."

I shuffle closer to her, confused and a bit embarrassed, and she reaches out and pulls me between her legs.

The kiss is different from anything I've ever felt before, and I feel myself stirring. She has one arm around my waist, holding me close to her, and I both feel and hear my zipper being lowered.

"You want to please your teachers, don't you, Allen?"

And then I lose all control, although there's nothing I need to control. She's doing it all. Doing to my dick what I've been doing myself, in the shower and late at night in my bed.

She's telling me how big I am—and I certainly feel bigger down there than I've ever felt before—and she's purring about what a hunk I am.

I'm inside her. She's wet and warm. She's clutching my butt cheeks and pressing and releasing and I'm moving in and out of her. The friction is driving me crazy, and I feel tight and the buildup of my spunk all at once.

She's saying how she loves how I play the innocent but am so good at it that I must be fucking all of the women—and that all of the women must love being fucked by me. She's making animal noises and groaning like I'm hurting her, although she declares that I'm not.

I shudder and come. And then, in total embarrassment and fear, I push off from her and go running out of the room. I'm half way down the hall before I remember that I'm hanging out and stop to adjust my pants. Luckily, there's no one else there.

Tomorrow I think I'll get my English class changed. I can't bear the thought of sitting there in class and having her look at me—and knowing and, worse, maybe asking me to her office again. I check my feelings, but other than shooting off, I feel more fear—and disgust, and not all with myself—than any of the feelings I thought I'd feel.

* * * *

It's mid September. It's been a hot year, though, and it looks like the summer temperatures will go right into October. That's been good for my mowing service. I've managed to work that around my classes, and I think, with the extensiveness of the warm weather, I'll manage to cover the tuition cost for the full year.

Grandma's in the hospital, and Grandpa's spending most of the days there. I pretty much have to batch for myself now. Grandpa has told me that I'd better learn to cook and wash for myself, because it won't be long until I'm on my own—without anyone being able to do anything about that.

"You're going to have to be making more of your own decisions from now on," he told me.

I restrained myself from doing cartwheels. I'm sure he thought that would scare me, but ever since that encounter with Miss Rogers—and it bringing to mind the magazines at Mr. Crabtree more than anything I'll bet she wanted me to be thinking about—I've been worrying my mind over what I'm interested in, what I want. And I don't think that either Grandma or Grandpa would like to know what I've been thinking.

* * * *

I'm at Mr. Crabtree's, just finishing up his lawn. It isn't all that hot today, but I'm not wearing a T-shirt anyway. I'm not quite sure why I'm not doing that. I'm less sure of why I've worn gym shorts that ride low on my hips. But I suspect it has something to do with the way Mr. Crabtree is sitting there on his porch, watching me mow, and about what's been on my mind

16

recently. He's in gym shorts too—and he isn't wearing any T-shirt either. And he's got a really, really finely worked body.

I feel all tingly and I'm hard down there. I know this is exactly what Grandma doesn't want me feeling or doing, but I'm feeling pretty free and euphoric. I like this feeling. I like it a lot.

"You're done?" Mr. Crabtree calls from the porch?

"Yes. Not too hard today," I call back. "It's getting cooler. That takes the strain off."

"That and you've mowed all summer," he says. "Your body's hard now."

He's not looking at my face. His gaze has gone down from my pecs to below my waist, and that doesn't change a thing in my arousal.

"Lookin' real good . . . real good," he continues, as he lifts his gaze to connect with mine and smile. "Come on up and have something to drink."

He stands as I climb the stairs to his porch. He's already got a pitcher of iced tea out here today.

"Unless you'll have a beer," he says, as he gestures at the tea. I see the magazines, as usual, are strewn on the table beside where I sit.

I also see something else. I see that his gym shorts are tented. I am aware that mine still are too—and I'm aware of that because I see where Mr. Crabtree's gaze has gone again.

I clear my throat. "I believe today I'll take you up on that offer of a beer, if it's just the same to you."

He smiles at me. It's a big smile, like we've made a step toward something he's been working on for some time. And, in fact, maybe we have.

"I don't have any out here," he says, holding the smile. He's moved his hand down to the waist of his gym shorts, which are pulled down in front because of that tenting. He sticks his thumb under the waistline and pulls them down a bit more. I can see the line of the curve under his flat belly and the creases on either side where the thighs meet the hips, dipping down toward the still-hidden center of him. I feel my breathing coming a little harder.

"If it's beer we want, we'll have to go inside. Will you come inside with me?"

"Yes, that would be fine," I say. It comes out more a squeak than anything else, though.

He smiles and backs up to the door, never taking his eyes off me, and pulls the screen door open. The other door into his kitchen is already open.

"Go on through to the living room," he says as I move past him. My shoulder brushes against his chest as I pass. It makes me shudder. I've felt the downy hair he has running on the underside of his well-muscled pecs. I'd already seen that the line of fine, curly hair came together on his sternum and moved down his belly, where it flared out as it disappeared under his waistband. With his gym shorts pulled down in front, I have seen that there is thicker hair curling up from beneath the waistband in front.

"I'll just be a minute," he says. "Just getting us a couple of beers from the frig."

I walk—almost stumble—on through to the living room, my trembling increasing as I go. I have no experience in this. This all could be natural. This might not be what I want to think it is. And I might not be able to go through with it even if it is. But I feel so ready for it. I've been like a bird in a cage all these years. I feel like I'm busting to do something. I thought maybe with women—but with Miss Rogers, there really was nothing. But what would Grandma say? How disappointing it will be to . .
.

Screw Grandma, I think as I sink down on his sofa. Then I give a nervous little laugh. Grandpa said I had to make my own decisions now. And about time I did that. But what if I'm wrong?. Just how embarrassing that would be. And then what? What then in life? Do I go looking for something? How would I do that? I know nothing. I'm not prepared for anything like . . .

And then I see that I haven't been wrong at all. I haven't misread any signals. And knowing that makes me tremble even more than when I wasn't sure.

Mr. Crabtree is walking across the dining room, toward me. He has a can of beer lifted out in each hand. But that's all he's wearing. He's naked. And his dick is huge and hard and curved up. And he's walking like he's proud of his body, as well

18

he should be. He's a Greek god. And he's walking like I know exactly what's going on and what I'm here for.

But I don't know. I mean I know why I think I'm here and I know what I think I want. But beyond that, I know nothing. What am I supposed to do now? Grandma would say I'm supposed to stand up and walk out of the house and just keep on walking.

But he's standing there in front of me, holding a can of beer out to me and smiling. Not a hint of doubt in his mind. Have I given him the impression that I know more about this than I do—that I'm fully sold on this? What should I do now?

But I don't really have to do anything. I take the beer. My hand is shaking so bad I'm afraid the beer will slosh out of the can.

"Don't be scared," he says. "I'm going to treat you right. I've waited all summer for this."

"I don't know. I'm not sure . . . ," I squeak.

"I walked into this room naked and erect and you're still here, aren't you?"

"Yes," I croak.

"So that means you know."

He takes a deep draw from his beer can, and, mimicking him because I can't think of anything else to do, I do the same with mine.

Then he takes the can from me and sets both of them down on the coffee table. And in one fluid motion he sits down close beside me; puts an arm around my shoulders; and, cupping the back of my head, brings my mouth to his and pushes his tongue between my lips. His taste is beery, that isn't a bad taste. His other hand is palming my belly, which feels like jelly under his touch. But it doesn't stay there long. It goes directly to my basket, grabbing my dick through the material of the gym shorts. I, of course, am still hard. Which tells him all he wants to know—about what I want and what he can do with me.

Although all of my senses are pinging off those two locations—his tongue inside my mouth and his hand gripping my dick, my mind is racing. What am I supposed to do? Where do my arms go. Am I supposed to reach for his crotch too?

In the event, I'm immobile. And Mr. Crabtree doesn't seem to care. He's doing what he wants to do, and I'm not resisting. So, for him it's all good.

I have to say that, as guilty as I now feel, so far it's all good for me too. This despite the voice of Grandma in the background telling me just to pull away, stand up, and get the hell out of there. I can even hear her voice screaming, "Get the hell out of there!"

He grips my hair and tugs my head back. I feel the pain of it, but it's exhilarating. And it's offset by the sensation of his lips now at the hollow of my neck. And then on my throat. On my right nipple. His teeth tug at the nipple and the rumble of a whimper comes up from my belly and I groan. I hear him laugh deep in this throat, and then he's working the other nipple.

His hand is under the waistband of my shorts, gripping my dick, flesh to flesh. How in the hell . . . when did he . . . ? I moan deeply.

"Please, please," I whimper.

"Yes, I'm going to be very good to you," he murmurs. "I'm going to fuck you good. Young stud. Love fucking young studs. I can do you good."

Has he misunderstood me? What in the fuck did my plea mean anyway? He said fuck. *I* said fuck. Oh shit. He's going to fuck me. He's going to fuck me! Oh shit, oh shit! I pant hard and moan deeply. He's slow-stroking my cock. Just the way I liked to do it. Just the way that aroused me the most, the fastest, when I did it myself. But someone else is doing it. A man. Not a boy, a man. Magnificent body. Could fuck anyone. Wants to fuck me. It means a lot that the guy doing me has a good body.

"We'll take our time," he says. "I'll do you right."

His dick's going to be inside me. Can I take it? How much pain? It's huge. Did you see it? It's a monster. You who? I'm hyperventilating. He's going to stick all of that inside me. Oh god, what am I doing?

I only now realize that I have a hand wrapped around his cock. He's breathing hard now too. He's moaning now too. I take my hand away, but only by commanding it to do so in my mind. And my hand has a mind of its own. Rather than withdrawing, it has laced his balls between its fingers and is gently tugging on them.

"Oh shit, yes," he moans. "You're good at this. We're gonna have fun. I'll fuck you good, baby."

Good at this? I've never done anything like this before.

His hand leaves my cock and I feel that arm coming around under my waist, as he moves lower on my body. My torso is twisted toward the arm of the sofa, and I lose contact with his balls and, not knowing what else to do with my arms, I raise them over my head and dig my fingers into the underside of the sofa arm that my head is now resting on. I arch my back and gasp as he takes a nipple in his teeth again. He lifts and tugs at my torso, pulling me into a reclining position along the line of the sofa. He's crouched over me on his hands and knees. I like what I see in the curving and bulging of his muscles. I'm glad the guying doing me first has a great body—a man's body.

His mouth moves down my sternum to my belly button, where his tongue does a darting in and out tease. Both of his arms come away and his hands are at my waistband, pulling the shorts and jock strap down and off my legs. He lifts my right leg up and moves it to the other side of his torso, trapping it against and rising up the back of the sofa.

He scrapes the fingernails of both hands down my chest and belly while taking my dick inside his mouth, and I arch my back and give a gasp and a little cry at the twin shocks and pleasure of these sensations. He sucks the bulb of the cock hard and I groan loudly. He is humming and I can feel the vibrations all through my body. His lips slide down the sides of the dick, once, twice, three times. My arms arc down to grabbing the back of his head.

I don't know if I'm trying to hold him to my crotch or force him away. The sensation of his sucking is overwhelming. I had no idea it would be like this. I had no idea how much pleasure could be gotten from it. If this is fucking, fucking is heaven.

But this isn't really fucking. Not yet.

He's tugging on my balls with one hand. His other hand glides up my body to my chin. A thumb is at my lips, and I suck it in, slurping it. Not knowing in the least what I should be

21

doing, but knowing from the sounds he's making that he's happy with how it's going.

But he's going to fuck me. He's going to stick that big thing up inside me—and pump. He'll rip my guts out.

"Please, please," I whimper again.

He takes that as a request to pump his mouth harder on my cock. Down. Gasp. Up, groan. Repeat. His slick fingers are at my rear entrance. I start involuntarily to buck as they enter me. I feel crammed, full, and I've seen those fingers. And I've seen that much bigger cock. He's going to stick that inside me. Oh shit. Oh, fuccck! What's that the fingers are rubbing? I've read about the prostate. I've read what you can do with it. I never knew. Oh, fuccccck!

"I'm going to come!" There's no way he understood me. His thumb is stifling any ability I might have had to form words properly

I'm writhing, bucking, trying to let him know he's taking me beyond any control I might have.

And then I come.

He rises off me, laughing, cum dribbling down his chin. He rises over my body and goes into a deep kiss. I have my own cum in my mouth. It should be disgusting. It isn't, though. I suddenly feel very weary, glad that it's over but satisfied too—in a way I've never felt satisfied before. My cum tastes salty. Not much more I get from it than that.

But it's not over.

"God, I like them young. Young stud like you will be up for it in a couple of minutes again," he mutters and then he laughs.

And then he is crouching over me again, but our bodies reversed. His hands are rolling my butt up and his head is disappearing between the orbs. I feel his tongue run down into my crease and find the rim of my entrance.

I pant and moan. His cock pokes at my cheeks and my eyes. Then he finds my lips and I have little choice but to open to it and start doing whatever I can imagine is done in sucking a cock. He's not objecting.

I'm lost for several minutes with my attention focused both on what he's doing at my ass entrance and my attempts to accommodate and suck on his cock. How long has this gone on? How much longer? How much arousing pleasure can I get? Can I give?

He turns me on my belly along the couch, with him sitting beside my waist. I don't know where they've come from, but there is a string of attached condom packets on the coffee table and a bottle of what I assume is lubricant. I'm still trying to regularize my breathing, but I just can't bring it under control.

I watch him in fascination as he opens a packet, extracts a condom, and rolls it on his cock. "Yes, going to do you real good. Fuck you to heaven. Beautiful young body," Mr. Crabtree is muttering as he slathers lubricant on his sheathed cock.

This isn't helping to regularize my breathing.

He's going to fuck me. With that huge cock. "Jump up and run!" I hear the voice of my Grandma. "It's not too late!"

But if I do that, it might be too late for what I think I want in life. There's got to be pleasure in it. Maybe not the first time. But eventually. There are guys who want it. Who beg for it. Again and again.

"Please, please," I whimper.

"Want it, don't you? Can't wait for it. Sweet body. Bet it's a sweet, tight hole. We're going to have fun. Ream you a wider channel than any of your buddies have."

He crouches over me on the sofa and turns me on my back under him. I can't help it; I run my hands over his bulging biceps and under his pits to his pecs. And down his torso to his cock. Our cocks close together. I hold them together in a thick bundle and stroke, as he comes in for another kiss.

Pulling away from the kiss, he laughs a low laugh and yes, "Yes, you are so ready for it."

He turns me on my belly again underneath his crouching body. An arm snakes under my waist, pulling me up on my knees. A wet feeling at my entrance and then inside, the fingers digging, pushing lube inside. Feeling totally full. And those are just the fingers. He's going to fuck me with that cock. Ream my channel wide.

I cry out and writhe under him. "Oh shit! Oh fuck!"

"That's just the bulb," he says in my ear, his chest pressing on my shoulder blades, an arm still under my waist.

23

"Oh god, take it slow, please!" I warble. "I've never before . . ."

"What? You've never been fucked in the ass before?"

"No, none of it. None of what we've done."

"Oh, sweet jesus. Want me to stop?"

"No, please. I want it. I know it will hurt. Just . . . just go slow."

"Oh, fuckin' A. The first time? For real? Oh, sweet fuck. I love to get them fresh, but I rarely . . . oh, fuckin' sweet jesus. OK, we'll go slow. I'll treat you right baby. I'll be good to you. When I've done you, you'll want it again and again."

"Just give me time."

"I'm already half in, baby. My talking was to distract you."

I hold my breath and stiffen. I can feel him deep inside now. He didn't lie. It's in me. God, it's at least half in me. I've got a huge dick inside me. He's doing it. I'm taking it. I've taken a huge cock! I can do this!

"Breathe, baby, breathe. And relax. Yes, like that. Widen your stance. We'll tighten up again later. Yes, like that. See, you can take it. It's good for you, baby. Daddy's good for you."

"It hurts like hell," I whimper.

"Do you want me to . . . ?"

"Just make the hurt go away. Tell me it won't always be like this. Tell me it will be good."

"After this, you'll want it inside you all the time, baby. And I'm all in now. We'll rest for a minute and then we'll really be doing it and the pain will go away and all there will be is the pleasure."

"And the knowledge that I took it. That I have it all inside me," I whimpered.

"Yes, that too, sweet baby. Yes, that too, now, here we go."

I grit my teeth and try to suppress the scream as he starts to slow pump inside me.

"What a fuckin' sweet ass."

He is right. At length the pain drifts at least half way into pleasure. He keeps promising me it will get better and better. And he keeps pumping. Faster and faster. Pain, but I don't care.

24

I'm lost to it, slamming my butt back to meet his thrusts, cum building up inside me—and . . . shooting off . . . again.

He keeps pumping. When he's ejaculated, he takes his arm out from under my waist and I collapse on the cushions. He lowers his body at a full stretch on my back and moves his hands around my body, stroking me.

"See, Fuckin' young stud. You're getting hard again. I'm gonna need more time, though. What a sweet fuck."

He turns my face to his and we kiss.

"That was one Grade A fuck, Allen, my boy. You were worth the summer investment. The beers gotta be too warm to drink now. I'll go get fresh ones. Then we'll fuck again. You'll like it even more the next time. And you'll love it the time after that."

Fuck again? I whimper wearily, not being sure whether that idea scares me or exhilarates me. Maybe both. And maybe that's part of the thrill of it.

* * * *

Both Grandma and Grandpa are in a home now. I visit them almost daily. I have the house all to myself and I'm doing well enough financially to stick with the junior college. My grades are good enough that I'll be able to transfer at the end of the semester this summer. I think I'll go to the university that I can commute to from here.

I like the freedom of having a house to bring guys back to. The table my feet go under is my own now. The men I bring back here usually are older men in their early or mid thirties. I meet them in bars. I always let them make the first move. I don't want anybody who doesn't want me so much that they'll make the moves. I like the older men. They have experience and they're still young enough to have a vigorous stroke. I like to have it deep and strong. And I like to have it big. I'm still enthralled with the idea of having something that big inside me—wanting to be there, needing to be there. And they are grateful a younger guy like me will give them a fuck. Some are so grateful that they are generous. That's helped me stay afloat.

They've got to have good bodies, though. Of course I've had few with as good a body as Mr. Crabtree had.

I haven't been back to Mr. Crabtree's since last October. I don't regret him one bit and I would have kept on. But it turns out that he likes guys that are fresh. By the time mowing season was over last year, I could tell that he was itchy to move on. He's engaged a guy right out of high school to do his lawn this summer—and, no doubt, to be done by him before the summer is over.

My big project now is that I'd like to find my mother and see what she's doing—and just decide for myself how bad that is.

Best Job in the World

"What a crock of crap this is," Philip Metcalf muttered to himself—there being no other figure in his plush office overlooking the activity on the editorial floor below him through a bank of glass windows. "And I think we've used this title a hundred times before. Just how gullible can our readers get? How did Tony let this one get past him?"

He held up the grainy cover of one of his company's best-selling pulp sex mags and peered at the title "My Life as a Male Pole Dancer" that was blazoned in screamy red lettering half way down the contents list.

He flipped open the magazine to the article and read, "Who would have guessed that a corn-fed lad from Iowa would wind up . . . ?"

Just the usual shit; a country hick waving his booty on some dive's bar and calling it sexy, Philip thought. We don't run pics on his sort of trash anymore. Tony's lost all touch with whatever creativity and sense of the fresh he'd ever had. For the third time today, the publisher of the chain of girlie and homo rags contemplated firing his managing editor. But he knew that Tony probably did have a good feel for the readership. He also knew that firing Tony would require finding another managing editor. And doing that would interfere with Philip's golf game. This has gotta be the shittiest job in the world, Philip thought.

He slapped the magazine down on the expansive, shiny top of his mahogany desk and picked up the letter sitting next to the magazine. "I can't think you enuff for running my story. It make me feel like a millun bucks," it began. "I seen your photo in a magasine, and I think you are a very handsum man. I wish there was some way I could show my gratude for . . ."

I didn't even notice this story in the magazine until I got this letter, Philip fumed. And when I went down and reamed Tony after I had seen, he just gave me a wary look and said he'd handled it. Having the hay seed pole dancer ask for an appointment to see me was Tony's idea of "fixing it?" This I gotta see.

Philip snorted and dropped the letter. He couldn't bring himself to read any more. Illiterate. The guy couldn't even write a letter. How had any story he had written ever gotten to be published—even in one of Philip's rags? But the hilarious spelling of the letter had been exactly why Philip hadn't shunted the appointment back downstairs when the guy had called in, wanting to see him. Maybe he'd get Tony up here and lower the boom on them both at the same time.

"This has got to be the world's crappiest job," he murmured. With a sigh, he reached over and punched the intercom button on his telephone. "OK, Vicky, you can tell the guy out there to come in now."

Philip was somewhat taken aback by the handsome, blond, neatly dressed young man who entered his office, carrying some sort of electronic device under his well-muscled arm. He'd expected some sleazy dirt bag chewing on a strand of oats.

"Listen, son," he said, as the smiling young man, looking at the same time both innocent and fetching with the lock of blond hair swirling down to his pale-blue eyes, walked to the desk and placed a boom box on the top, "if this is about

28

payment for the story, we don't pay for three months, and you should address all queries on that to . . ."

"You're even better in person than in the photos, Mr. Metcalf. I do want to thank you for running my story, and I've thought of how I hope I can thank you the right way. The guy downstairs I showed the story to certainly liked the way I thanked him for accepting it."

His voice was soft and rich. It had some sort of twang to it, which Philip thought might be Iowa. But who was he to know? He hadn't been any further west from Jersey City than Philadelphia. The young man was so good looking, though, and seemed so assured of himself that Philip was at a loss for words and just sat there, mesmerized, as the young man pushed a button on the boom box, causing music—pretty loud music with a strong bass beat—to boom forward.

Philip's eyes followed the young man as he moved with arresting, mincing steps back to the office door, shot the lock home with a sharp click, and then moved from window to window overlooking the editorial floor below, and snapped the blinds shut.

He turned and gave Philip a smile and a provocative look, and Philip sank into his plush executive chair and gave a little groan. It was beginning to dawn on him why Tony had agreed to run the guy's story—and also why sending the guy up to see him was how Tony thought the problem would be taken care of. It quite evidently wasn't the sweet young thing's writing that was convincing about his story's worth.

The young man obviously was in full control. Philip hadn't imagined this would go this way. He wouldn't have let him in for an appointment at all except that he had been looking forward to seeing what an illiterate, corn-fed country yokel from Iowa looked like as comic relief on an otherwise dull day.

The young man's hips started swaying and he pulled his polo shirt over his head.

Philip sucked air. The guy was really cut—ripped. He wasn't muscle bound, but every muscle was in place, fully developed, and part of a luscious package. His smooth, tanned torso was moving with the beat of the music, and his pecs were flexing and releasing right on the beat.

29

"My name in the magazine is listed as 'Charles,' but you can call me Chucky."

Of course I can, Philip thought, anything he could actually say, though, caught in his throat, which was constricting. He could feel a low growl of lust building from the center of his chest, busting to break out, but trapped inside by air moving in the wrong direction.

"All my friends call me Chucky, and we're going to be very good friends, you and me, I think. The man downstairs was happy to be my friend. He liked my story enough to print it. So I think you'll like me too. And I got lots of ideas for stories. I bet this will make a good story too." Chucky laughed. Philip couldn't manage much more than a gurgle.

Oh, god, I hope so, Philip thought. Chucky had pulled two long, red silk scarves from somewhere, and he was using them to dance in place with. Philip's eyes followed the slide of the scarves as Chucky moved them provocatively around and across his smooth, lightly tanned torso.

When Chucky reached down and jerked off his breakaway pants with one swift movement, Philip gasped, and a hand involuntarily went to his basket, which was already tenting out.

"Do you like me?" Chucky asked in a low, melodic voice. "Do you think I make a good story?"

All Philip could muster in reply was a low, guttural sound rising up from his gorge. His eyes were popping out at just how exotic—and suggestive—were Chucky's undulating movements to the beat of the boom box music. And he was reminded yet again how much better this was in real life than just reading fantasies about it and looking at photographs depicting it in the magazines he published. He sometimes got so bogged down in the tiring, dull business end of selling sex that he forgot what got him into this business.

He reached over and punched the intercom button and managed to croak. "Hold all of my calls for now, Vicky."

"Sure thing, Mr. M.," the intercom chirped back. Vicky had worked here a long time, and Vicky was no dummy. The rags in Metcalf's empire featured photos as well as written stories, and the auditions for a lot of those were conducted right here in Philip's office.

Of course, before now Philip had always been in complete control of what happened in this office. This was a whole new sensation for Philip. Maybe that's why it was turning him on as high as the volume of the boom box music.

As Philip buzzed off, Chucky was coming around the side of the desk. Standing behind Philip's chair, he pulled it away from the desk toward the large plate-glass window behind. Philip tilted his head back to find himself staring into a pert and nubby nipple on a very nicely developed, smooth-skinned chest.

He groaned. This wasn't anything like looking at one of the photos in his magazine. It had been so long since he'd auditioned guys for those photos that he'd forgotten the difference between a photo and the sensation of the guy actually being there. At the feel of Chucky's touch on his arm, Philip looked down and dumbly watched Chucky firmly wrap his forearm against the arm of his chair with one of the red silk scarves, holding his arm bound there. His head swiveled around to see Chucky doing the same to the forearm resting on the other chair arm.

In everything, the surprise and shock of what was happening—as pleasant as it was—kept Chucky one step ahead of him. Philip couldn't think of what he should say or do before Chucky had moved on to something else—something even more provocative than he had done before. And now the "do" was too late if he wanted to regain control. He was firmly bound to his chair.

Chucky came in front of him and moved in close, with Philip's knees between his thighs. The young man was still dancing in place, his torso slowly undulating in the most provocative way. Philip's eyes ran down the enticing line of Chucky's torso to the bulge of the red silk thong, which was all Chucky was now wearing.

"Gah, gah," Philip managed from his nearly paralyzed throat. But that was all he managed to say, fully realizing it was gibberish, before Chucky leaned over him, pulled Philip's head toward his face by pulling on Philip's tie, and having Chucky's minty-flavored mouth capture his.

31

Philip shuddered. The bulge between Chucky's legs was rubbing against Philip's crotch now—but the red thong was gone.

This was real. This wasn't just one of the lame, same-same stories being run in his magazine. Literacy and spelling and word usage didn't mean shit here.

Philip wasn't able to concentrate on the kiss—as arousing as he was finding it—because Chucky was already unbuttoning his shirt and running his hands in to grope Philip's chest and rub and tweak his nipples. And the arousal of this was quickly replaced with the sensation and sound of his belt buckle being undone and his zipper lowered and then of warm hands on his half-engorged and quickly hardening cock. The feel of Chucky's hard cock against Philip's belly made him hyperventilate. And he barely had time to appreciate Chucky's fisting of his shaft when he was gasping and gulping at the feel of a condom being rolled onto his cock and lubricant being slathered on the sheathed shaft.

A strangled "Muffff" sound and the bulging of his eyes as the pale blues of Chucky's bored into them and Chucky worked to get his tongue to the back of Philip's throat were the most reaction Philip could manage—other than the jerking and trembling of his body at every point, as Chucky, still weaving his torso to the beat of the boom box, slowly descended his channel on Philip's cock, rose, descended, rose . . . descended.

Racing through Philip's brain in constant, ear-ringing repetition was just one phrase: "God, this is the best job in the world."

Chucky was right. More of his stories would be bought for the magazines. And Philip knew just who could become his editor to make them readable.

Lance's Secret

Nearly every college fraternity house on the North American continent has one. At some it's a cook or a cleaner or a coed at the college—or a townie slut from across the tracks. In some it's the cougar mother of a frat brother whose family lives in town and who only was rushed by the fraternity because his mother was half-decent looking and put out like a rabbit. Typically, this individual is called the house punch. When it's a male, though, as it is at the Digamma Theta Theta fraternity house at the Calgary, Canada, university, he's called the house reliever.

At the Calgary DTT, the house reliever's name was Lance. Lance was brought in in perpetual pledge status purely for his reliever duties. It was a jock fraternity, where the dumbest but hunkiest of the team animals were put together with a team of smart guys whose duty it was to get all of the important athlete brothers just over the bar of passing each semester. The alumni would do anything for these athletes that they could get away with. They even paid the fees for a house reliever.

Lance was a student in the dental college, and he was lucky to get into any fraternity, as the dental students were considered the nerdiest and most obnoxious of any of the students in the university. Lance was a model of this rather than an exception. He'd been there six years on a four-year program thus far and still had trouble remembering how a mouth and teeth were supposed to work for anything but a blow job. This didn't stop him from trying to be the authority on any topic, of course, and the only recourse the fraternity brothers had when he got wound up on a topic he knew nothing about was to stuff his mouth with cock. That calmed him down, and he obviously enjoyed it. Some thought he even avoided taking his degree so he could stay in the DTT house as the reliever.

Lance knew blow jobs. And that was the full extent of Lance's duties at the DTT house—to relieve the tensions of the frat brothers who found they had awakened with a hard-on, or had built one up for the date that had fallen through that evening, or had slipped a porn DVD in the machine to take a break from the mind-numbing demands of adding 5 and 2 for their take-home math quiz, had raised a boner they couldn't get to go down, and had a class to go to. Lance was made for times like this. His name would be bellowed, and before the echo died out, Lance would scurry in, kneel in front of the needy 250-pounds of muscle and steroids, shape his mouth in a perfect O, and relieve the frat brother of his tensions.

Invariably, Lance would whine to be ass fucked as well, but the DTT frat brothers would have nothing to do with that. They were strictly hetero, they declared. When they wanted to fuck, they strutted down the campus walks until some coed, woman professor, or townie nymphet pulled them into the bushes and rode their cocks to lift off. DTT was the frat house for the hulking hunks. They had no need for a scrawny little ass like that of the pimply faced Lance. He was just there for occasional tension relief. There was nothing fag about a blow job received—or so the DTT men proclaimed. And no one contradicted them, the university woman not wanting them to think they were anything but hetero stud muffins. Thus, no one even dared mouth the word "bi" around the DTT guys—because everyone knows there's just hetero and homo and nothing in between.

Lance probably wouldn't have been kept around at all, except that his whining could be effectively stopped by stuffing his mouth with a plump man sausage—and all had to concede that he really did know how to give a blow job. What was really irritating about Lance, though, couldn't so easily be taken care of like his silly arguments about stuff he didn't know anything about could. Lance liked to wear short, wool plaid skirts—and nothing else. This would be a lot less of an irritant if he was built like the other, athletic frat brothers. But he was such a scrawny little thing—and was so whiny and mouthy when his throat wasn't stuffed—that the frat brothers, used to plump, luscious pussy, could only stay around him long enough to get their relief and then they were drop kicking him into the next room.

"Lance, dude, why you wearin' that damn short skirt again? It makes you look sure as hell silly, even though it goes with the way you mince around here and strike poofter poses."

"It's not a skirt, George," Lance would say with pursed lips, hands on hips and looking slightly wounded and Bette Davisish. "It's a kilt. Can't you tell by the tartan plaid? This is the Baird pattern. I'm Scottish. I'm Scottish proud."

"You ain't no Scottish guy, Lance. And you ain't no Baird either. You're Canadian. Well, not real Canadian. And your last name be Trubouche and you come from Montreal. So, if you anything, you just a little Frenchie prick. Now git you mouth over here and do me right."

Not more than thirty minutes later, there'd be a bellow from the other end of the frat house, and Lance would be swinging his little hips and sashaying over there to relieve Spike or Harold or Steve.

"God, Lance, if you shimmy in here one more time just in that skirt, I think I'm gonna upchuck. You on your way to a sickos' costume party or something?"

"No. It's Scotland Day, and I'm celebrating my heritage."

"You're no Scot, Lance. Lance," Harold said again. Then he giggled. "Lance. Lance. Lance. What sort of fuckin' fag name is that?"

"I'll have you know that there were lairds of Scotland named Lance." The indignant Lance stretched himself up to his full five foot four height of sagging flesh.

"Queens, more like," Harold said, a chuckle still tickling the back of his throat. "Lance. Lance. Lance. It just makes me see pink tutus, not Scottish kilts, whenever I say that name—and I'll bet it isn't Scotland Day, either. You're such a liar and know nothing. I don't think you're even capable of seeing the truth, let alone speaking it. Now get your whiny little ass over here and unhinge your jaw. Big one incoming."

"My ass?" Lance asked hopefully. "You know I'd just loved to be ass fucked by a big bruiser like you, Harold. Would you like to see what's under my kilt?"

"Oh, shit no. Spare me that. And look what you've done now. I'm not even at half staff anymore. Just the thought of fucking your whiny little butt. Get the hell out of here. And next time I call for you, don't be wearing a skirt and only use your mouth for what I need."

No matter what the frat brothers did to try to make Lance not wear those kilts, or to put on more clothes, or just not to lie or pontificate on what he didn't know with everything he said, it just didn't work. He was either stubborn or too dumb to get it—or, most likely, both. No one ever accused Lance of being the ripest banana in the bunch.

Lance slept in the pledges' dormitory at the top of the DTT house, in the attic, which was just one big room with a sloping ceiling set at weird angles. There were eight military cots for eight pledges. Counting Lance, though, there were nine pledges. There were only eight pledge slots each year, but Lance was only a pledge in name on the record books. This was the fourth year of his one-year pledge period. Lance's only reason for being here was to rap his mouth around a frat brother's fat cock when he was summoned to do so.

Lance slept on a pad at the end of the last pledge cot in the room. The rule for him when he was in the pledge dormitory and any other pledge was there was that he had to move around on all fours like a dog. That wasn't a punishment, though. Lance enjoyed that. In fact, he worked the pledge class real hard, begging to be fucked like a dog in the dormitory. But the pledge

36

class was made up of hulking hunks too. Except for when they need an emergency blow job, they all got their rocks off in the bushes with any number of willing young women just like their older frat brothers did.

To a man, they disdained Lance—and especially those kilts he wore, his whiny questions about who wanted to see what he wore under there, and his obsession with lying and pontificating about everything.

For some time in this pledge year session, the pledges didn't realize how much time Lance spent on the computer in the back corner of the dormitory when no one else was around. It was only the afternoon when the pledge Eric was coming into the dormitory when George bellowed for blow job service from two floors below and Lance popped up from behind the computer and ran downstairs that any of the pledges knew what Lance was doing on the computer. And it wasn't his dental school homework.

"Hey, come look at this, Cliff," Eric called to a pledge brother who was just coming up the stairs. "You gotta see what Lance has been looking at."

Within minutes five of the pledge brothers were gathered around the computer.

"What is that Web site?"

"It looks like some sort of big redneck guy's gay Web site. The name seems to be TruckinAnRammin. I think it's for truckers. And look at these threads on its forum. That's some pissy badmouthing. Some dude named Brassnkls is really whaling away at a bunch of truckers—calling them dirty faggots, poofters, and stuff and making fun of them—and they're all hissing back at him like a pit of snakes."

"So, who's this Brassnkls troublemaker?"

"It looks like it's our Lance. That's who he's checked in as. And boy is he acting like the world's toughest homophobe. Swinging in all directions in the middle of a gay truckers' forum, just seeing how much dust he can throw up into the air."

"Shhh. I think he's coming back," Clifford said. And the pledges scattered and worked at looking innocent.

When Lance came back into the room, he made the rounds of the five on his knees, asking if they wanted to see what he had under his kilt and begging them to give him a fuck.

It cleared the dormitory room in record time.

"I've had enough," Eric said to Clifford in the bushes next to the university chapel while the two were fucking coed twins.

"Well, go on then, I'm not done yet," Clifford answered.

"No, I don't mean this. I mean Lance lying all the time and begging for it while, out of the other side of his mouth, he's on line, pretending to be some hard-assed trucker homophobe when he's really a champion twinkle toes."

"So, what do you want to do about it?"

"Already started. I'll tell you when I'm finished in this pussy. Ahhhhhh, yes."

"You didn't," Clifford said that evening, when Eric pulled him over to the computer and showed him what he'd set up. Lance was downstairs whining loudly and declaring that he was the rightful queen of England, until George stopped up his mouth. Eric and Clifford decided then that they had at least fifteen minutes alone with the computer before Lance was finished sucking off George and would be coming upstairs.

"Yes, I did. Four of them live or drive near enough and took up the challenge."

"Four? How'd you get them to say they'd come?"

"I called them shitty names and followed them around the TruckinAnRammin Web site forum in the Brassnkls account name until I'd worked a bunch of them up to a frenzy, and then I challenged them to come and see if they could get a piece of me at this address."

"And they bit?"

"All four of them did. Set a time. Thursday at 4:00. Most of the brothers have practice then."

On Thursday at 3:45 Eric and Clifford, having made sure that only Lance would be in the house other than them, hid themselves in the dining room, off the communal living room. They barely made it into concealment before the doorbell rang and Lance was flouncing down the stairs in his little kilt to answer the door.

The trucker named Bubba had arrived early. Taken by surprise, Lance answered to the name Brassnkls when challenged. An uppercut to the chin and a fist to the solar plexus sent Lance reeling back onto the sofa in the living room. When BigRick arrived only five minutes early, Lance was already bent over the arm of the sofa, his kilt gathered up around his waist, and Bubba working on trying to reach Lance's tonsils from the inside with his nine-inch dick.

"That Brassnkls?" BigRick asked.

"Yep," Bubba answered. "I got nine inches in the little prick. You got something you want in there too? Gonna teach this little poofter about fuckin' with me."

"You think he can take ten at the same time?"

"I don't see why not. He's a real big talker on the forum—and from how he talks there, I'll bet he's empty on the inside and that there's lots of empty space room in there for both of us."

"OK, Turn him then and make some room for my approach. Hey, what's that dangling little thing between his legs?"

"Think that's what he thinks is a dick."

"Sheeet. You think so?"

"Here we go."

"Oh shit. Oh god. Oh pleazzzze!"

The plaintive screaming undoubtedly was the voice of Lance.

"You think we should try to call it?" Clifford whispered to Eric in the other room.

"Naw, the little bastard liar deserves whatever they give him," Eric answered in a voice full of steal. "Maybe this will make him think twice about jackassing and jerking guys around just to be a prick from now on."

Two new voices could be heard in the living room now. Eric and Clifford could barely hear what they were saying over the sobbing and grunting and groaning Lance was throwing up at the living room ceiling.

"That Brassnkls, the poofter?" a new voice said.

"Yep, Bubba answered. You here to give him your regards too?"

"Yep. Will there be anything left for us when yer done?"

"We'll see. Me and this guy both usin' his hole now, but one of you can take the mouth. Would be good to shut him up. After we're done, you two can have what we've got."

The fucking went on for a good half hour. Lance wasn't doing too much yelling or sobbing toward the end, though, and it progressively got quieter in the living room, accentuated eventually by four different expressions of ejaculation. When all Eric and Clifford could hear was low panting and soft moaning, they crept into the living room.

"He still with the land of the living?" Clifford asked.

"Yeah, looks like he's breathing," Eric said. And then he laughed. He sounded like he was trying to stifle it but just couldn't help himself.

"What?" Clifford asked.

"There, that," Eric said.

"What? I don't see anything."

"Yeah, that's the point. That little bump is the dick Lance has been telling us all he wanted to show us under that kilt of his. Talk about delusions of grandeur."

"Lance? He's that tiny and he calls himself Lance?"

The two shared a chortle.

"Well, no one ever questioned that Lance was delusional and thought a lot of himself without any reason," Clifford continued. "Do you think we should . . . ?"

"Shit!" Eric exclaimed.

"What?" Clifford asked.

"The little fucker's smiling. And he's humming."

And indeed Lance was smiling, but he wasn't humming; he was softly singing, "And am the queen of the universe, I am," in a monotone.

"The little prick enjoyed it," Eric declared, his voice laced with disgust.

"It . . . it . . . was . . . delicious," Lance murmured. Then he changed his tune. "Roll me over in the clover; roll me over and do it again, do it again. Roll me . . . Come on, boys, take me. I'm all yours."

"I can't take it," Eric cried out, and both he and Clifford fled up the stairs in defeat.

40

Emmet

We live in a university town, my wife and I, and we live in a neighborhood within five blocks of the edge of that university. It's an affluent neighborhood, built on heavily wooded, well-manicured lots on the side of a ridge, with narrow streets running up and down and twisting here and there. Almost like the country, but a wealthy enclave right in the small city. Quite staid we are. Not ones for quirkiness. Almost all of our neighbors work for the university in some academic or administrative capacity. I, for instance, teach English literature, and my wife teaches French literature. Both of us have held deanships but quickly gave those up, preferring to spend our time on our own studies rather than the squabbling of other professors.

At one time the house on every lot touching on ours, on either side and along the back was occupied by university couples. We serve in different departments, though, and both a university football team assistant coach and the women's basketball coach are living in the neighborhood, so our neighborhood gatherings aren't quite as stilted and inbred as our required-attendance departmental functions. On the whole, however, we're a pretty dull, vanilla bunch, full of pomp and circumstance and stuffy academic dignity.

Ours also is a pretty "in for the duration" neighborhood, university positions here being coveted and safe enough that, once acquired, they are not often given up. We've lived here nearly a decade now, and we are the next-to-newest residents for a block in any direction. It was the recent turnover in the house backing on the south side of our property that threw my world off balance.

When we moved in Wilfred Singleton lived in that house, a brick Dutch colonial with little back yard to speak of at all, which, however, was so overgrown when we moved in that we couldn't even see his house from ours—nor did we hear anything from that direction, even though we had a screened garden pavilion almost abutting the fence between the side of our lot and the back of his. So peaceful and inviting was the pavilion, which overlooked our flagstone garden, with a fishpond and trickling fountain, that I immediately claimed it as my writing study during the warmer months of the year. The pavilion had electricity, with Wi-Fi connection, a grouping of comfortable patio furniture at one end, and a table at the other end big enough for me to lay out my laptop and all of the research material I might need. We lived in the lower middle south, so I could work, sometimes until 3:00 am, in the pavilion with just the sound of the fountain, crickets, the frogs in the pond, and the ceiling fan lazily whop, whop, whopping overhead.

Singleton had been an economics professor at the university—quite a well-known one too. I had heard of him before we came to the university. But he was retired and was a recluse—and obviously had done little or nothing to keep up what had once been an extensive rock garden, teeming with azaleas, rhododendrons, hemlocks, and Japanese maples surrounding his house. I was actually surprised he was still alive, as I hadn't heard anything about him for several years before we moved in.

I was told that he had resigned his professorship and become a recluse some five years earlier, when his wife, a Spanish literature professor, had been hit and killed while she was out for an evening walk by a car on the winding, narrow road in front of their house.

I did see him now and again, standing among the clutter of his back yard, blinking his eyes and looking a bit lost, and we did exchange brief pleasantries on some of those occasions. I think he knew who I was, but he was always vague enough that I wasn't sure. My pavilion was set high enough off the ground that I could clearly see over the wooden fence separating our lots.

Last year about Christmas time, though, I heard sirens on his street. It was cold enough then that I was working in my study on the second floor, which had a window overlooking his lot. I could see the flashing red light on top of an emergency vehicle through the trees and, both curious and concerned, I walked around the corner to see what was happening.

Singleton was sitting on the tailgate of an ambulance and several other neighbors had already gathered around him. He was wrapped in a blanket, but I could tell that he otherwise was naked. He had the vacant stare of someone who just wasn't there.

"My husband called 911," a neighbor, who was the director of the university press, was telling a small group of people when I walked up. "Wilfred was just out on the street, stark naked, and screaming for a car to run him over. Poor dear. It's happened before, but never this bad. I guess now he'll have too . . ."

I retreated, having heard what I needed to hear and not wanting to intrude any further into Singleton's melt-down or the grief he never had seemed to be able to recover from. I thought this was all very sad, but I knew that the neighborhood would be relieved—that Singleton had become much too shocking and unconventional for the comfort of the community and that now, naturally, he would have to be put in a nursing home.

The house sat vacant until the late spring—and quiet except for the three weeks in the last part of March when a couple of middle-aged couples—probably Singleton's daughters and their husbands, went through an orgy of filling a dumpster in the house's driveway with what looked like perfectly good items. I remember nearly hyperventilating one day when standing at my study window and watching them toss in

Singleton's extensive collection of books. I was sure that a small fortune in research material—and most likely the makings of a core library for an economics department in some university—was going to the landfill. But the couples were from out of state and I'd never seen them there while Singleton was alive. So, I guess their lives and interests had not intersected with the professor's for some time.

I didn't think more about Singleton or that house until mid summer. We always went to either England or France in May and June, officially to continue our own studies, but really because we loved being in Europe so much. We crossed the Atlantic together, but often, once in Europe, my wife, Joanne, and I went our separate ways. We weren't a close couple, but we were compatible. We were both professors by the time we met, and both were people more focused on our individual lives and interests than on a significant other. But, teaching at the same university, we found we were comfortable with each other and we both had reached a stage in our life when we appreciated having a companion to share meals and discussion and little discoveries with. I suspected that Joanne was a lesbian, and, for all I knew, she was aware that I had only slept with men—seeking out a particular kind of man that would be an extra taboo where we now lived—and not even men for a few years before we married. At our stage of life it just didn't seem to matter. Not that we were old; we were both in our early forties. But because we were settled in our ways and happy with them. Or, in my case, resolved to be as happy as possible under the circumstances.

I'd kept my needs and wants private pretty successfully. In my twenties, I'd gone looking for what I wanted—and in some pretty dangerous areas. I don't think anyone who knew me now would guess at the peculiarity of what I wanted, what aroused me. As I'd gotten older and became more successful in academia, I increasingly realized that what I wanted just would not be acceptable in the world I was entering. I had wanted it so badly that I let myself be degraded to get it in my late twenties. As my career was firming up, I listened to myself when I was being satisfied the way I wanted to be. It wasn't dignified; it wasn't what a mature English literature professor should pant for. So, I slowly weaned myself off it. But I still wanted it. I couldn't deny that. Marrying and settling down in this university town—in this particular neighborhood—was part of my campaign to overcome my latent desires.

I noticed the difference next door when I came back to our university town in late June. I suddenly—and a bit distressingly—could clearly see the back and back garden of the Singleton house. To my eye, it had moved a good twenty feet closer to our lot line while I was in England. Joanne was still in France, having secured a sabbatical there. She wouldn't be home until the fall. So I was batching it. There was a glassed-in sun porch on the back of the Dutch colonial, an addition to the house that I hadn't even been fully aware of while Singleton was in residence, and I could clearly see into that from both my garden pavilion, when I stood up, and from one of the windows in my second-floor study in the house.

The house hadn't moved, of course. It just had sold and the new owners were having the gardens cleared, which made the house loom larger visually. And they were having a stone patio laid to cover all of the back yard except for the bushes and ornamental trees that were being kept.

It was several days after I returned that I espied any activity over there, though. It was the sound of a woman's voice on the telephone—a voice that carried and a conversation that was interspersed with lilting laughter—that brought me to the window of my study.

The garden room of the Dutch colonial had been transformed into a usable room. Whoever the new owners of the house were, they had traveled and had eclectic tastes. The room was furnished and had touches of both the Mediterranean and the Orient. There was a desk in a rich rosewood color that, from its carvings, was probably from China or Hong Kong. There were fan chairs; some brass work, perhaps from Turkey; and what appeared to be a double-bed-sized studio couch with a flamboyant Indian-design coverlet on it and a profusion of pillows in a myriad of textiles and patterns. As jumbled as the sun room space was, it all seemed to go together well.

Sitting at the desk was a trim brunette, perhaps in her late forties. She was having an animated conversation on the phone and doing much of her speaking with her hands. I doubted she had any idea her voice carried as well as it did. I had been sitting in my wing chair just in front of the window and trying to read some pretty difficult poetry passages in Middle English when I'had become aware of the level of sound coming from the Dutch colonial. Fully aware of it now, I found myself standing at the window, looking down into her back yard, and concentrating on what she was saying—and just not quite being able to catch the words. It might have been all right and I could have focused away from it on my own reading if I either couldn't discern any words at all or could clearly hear the conversation. But this middle ground just would not work.

Still standing at the window, I was becoming resolved to move to my wife's study at the other end of the bedroom wing, when my eyes caught movement outside of the neighboring house, in the garden. A man was there, working on clearing undergrowth in the far corner of the lot. He was black and not too young or too old, perhaps in his early thirties. He was tall and well built. Not heavy and not thin. But he was very well muscled. He was wearing shorts but otherwise was naked. The muscles of his arms and chest were well defined, tapering down to a slim waist and flat belly. He was an ebony black, but seemingly not of the American variety. He looked more Caribbean, the aspect of a Harry Belafonte or a Sidney Poitier. Which, to me, meant that he looked sensual and desirable.

I stayed at the window, watching his movements perhaps a moment too long, as, possibly sensing he was being watched, he looked up and saw me in the window. We both stood, transfixed, if for only a moment, and then he looked away and picked up a pair of hedge clippers and I turned away and went, almost reluctantly now, to my wife's study, my Middle English poems in hand.

Over the next few days, I caught glimpses of them both—the brunette woman on her telephone in the sun porch—and the Caribbean hunk working on the garden. Within days, other neighbors had told me about Cleo. She was an anomaly for the neighborhood, so I could sense the hiss in the conversations I heard about her. A single woman and not connected with the University. Some neighbors believed she worked in some sort of import-export business but also that she was independently wealthy. The rumor was that she had paid cash for the house.

I didn't ask about the young black man, and no one else mentioned him either. We were well enough down in the south that it wasn't unusual for black workmen to be around and about—and for people to not really "see" them. Certainly not discussed by the likes of us. There were black professors and athletic coaches at the university, of course, but they were considered to be in a different class altogether. Almost acceptable.

I can't say I didn't "see" this young man—I took every opportunity I could to get glimpses of him. But then, I wasn't the typical resident in this neighborhood, I didn't think. This despite how hard I'd tried to be just right for this neighborhood.

Beyond those little snippets on the new owner, Cleo, no one seemed to know much of anything.

The shock, torture, and glory of my life came at the end of that first week. I had eaten dinner late and watched a BBC Masterpiece Theater mystery in the downstairs den that was a quite large extension off the back of our house, projecting into our garden. Having finished with the TV later than was customary for me, I was later than usual coming up to my study to work on a lecture. I entered the room and was just about to turn on the light, when a familiar—but very out of place—series of sounds assaulted my ears. Rather than turn on the light I moved to the study's window on the side of the house and, from the dark room, looked down into Cleo's garden.

The lights were on full on her sun porch. Both she and the black gardener were naked. She was on her back on the studio bed, in full view, and was writhing while she grunted and groaned in that voice of hers that carried so well. The black gardener was crouched over her between her legs, holding them up and out with his fists, and rhythmically fucking her. He periodically dipped his mouth down to the nipples on her full breasts and gave suck, while she arched her back and grabbed his short-cropped head.

I stood at the window and watched the full performance. I felt my buttocks cheeks clinch and expand in the same rhythm as his as he pumped her. The undulating ebony muscles of his

47

back were glistening slightly with the effort of the fuck. He was a magnificent animal in full prime and conditioning. I felt my hand go to my engorging cock, and I held myself through the material of my trousers and stroked down the length of me with a thumb. And then back up, and down.

When he was done, he turned, casually picked up a pack of cigarettes from the desk and came over to the glass wall opposite my window perch and lit up. My breath, already ragged, caught in my throat, and I heard a low growl coming up from inside of me. He was horse hung. His muscled body perfectly proportioned but for the noticeably oversized, magnificent black cock and the low-hanging testicles, giving him almost a primeval aspect reminiscent of fertility rites.

Cleo, still spread-eagled on the studio couch was rubbing the fingers of one hand in the folds hiding her clitoris and working her nipples with the fingers of the other hand.

He was looking out into the night, and it seemed like he was looking up at where I stood at my window. Surely he couldn't see me there, but it certainly seemed that he could. And not just that he could see me but that he could see into, through me. That he knew that I wanted him inside me too. I could almost hear jungle drums in the background marking the exotic—and erotic—intrusion in our staid, very proper neighborhood.

I ached to be part of that tableau.

I gave a little cry as I ejaculated inside my pants. I drew away from the window, but I couldn't bring myself to leave the room. I withdrew only enough that there was no way that he could see me but that I could still see into the sun porch.

The young black man was masturbating himself with one hand while he smoked the cigarette down to its filter with the other. I unzipped my fly and pulled my cock out as well. It was a sticky mess, but that didn't prevent me from stroking it as I watched him stroking himself hard again—and felt myself getting hard again too.

In full, magnificent erection, he turned, stubbed out the cigarette in an ashtray on the desk, and returned to the studio couch. I watched, mesmerized, as he leaned down, put an arm under the waist of Cleo, and turned her, first, onto her belly, on

48

the studio couch, and then pulled her up to her knees. She let him manipulate her as he would. I watched in both shock and arousal, as he pushed that long, thick, black cock into her again—but this time into her ass. She writhed under him again and became quite vocal again. But they were exclamations of encouragement and satisfaction.

I turned and fled the room, seeking out the bathroom in my room—Joanne and I have both separate bedrooms and bathrooms—and barely made it in time before I ejaculated a second time into the toilet bowl.

I couldn't punish myself any further. I stripped, tossed my clothes in the hamper to wash early the next morning in considerable embarrassment, showered, went to bed naked—and masturbated myself to another ejaculation while visions of the black gardener's erect cock and the clinching muscles of his buttocks played over and over again in my head.

That was only the first of frequent sexual couplings I saw between Cleo and the black gardener on the porch, both during the day and at night. And I participated in all of the ones I observed.

Ours was an insular university town and our neighborhood an even more close-knit, conventional community. Within a week I'd heard the scoop on the young black man from a neighbor with mutual property lines to mine and that of Cleo's Dutch colonial.

That neighbor was southern town raised and bred and thus a bit breathless and scandalized by what she had to tell me over our shared hedges running between our driveways.

"He's living with her apparently. He introduced himself to me as Emmet. He says he's looking for work. It's her house, of course. She's the one with the job. And she's obviously older than he is."

After a few more days I had occasion to introduce myself to Emmet myself. He was serving wine for one of the wineries at a wine festival being held on the grounds of a historical plantation house only about three miles to the west of our neighborhood.

His voice was deep and rich. I knew it would be. He didn't seem at all surprised when I asked him if he lived at the address of the former Singleton house. It was as if he knew who I was and where I lived.

I was at a loss for words to have a coherent discussion with him, so I couldn't pursue my curiosity. But it seemed that he knew what I had seen—and how it had affected me.

When we shook hands, I felt the electricity. I wondered if he did too. And he might have, because he didn't let loose of my hand until someone nudged up at my elbow, wanting a wine tasting, and the liquid brown eyes of his that had been boring into my depths turned back to his current duties.

Another week after that I heard his voice on the local jazz and classical music station, and I confirmed in a discussion with him over the back fence when he was working in the garden, and I was, unsuccessfully, trying to work in the pavilion and ignore that he was working in the garden, that he had gotten a job—at least temporarily—at the local classical music radio station.

Stealing a march on the neighbors, I declared to all within blocks that I was having the neighborhood gathering for brunch on July 4th and went to considerable effort and expense to provision the affair, even though various neighbors were bringing this and that. We spread out between our large first-floor den opening out onto a covered patio, the flagstoned garden around the fish pond, and the screened garden pavilion.

The whole reason I'd gone to this trouble was to be with Emmet, even if I also had to be with twenty other assorted university professors and administrators. Cleo came and was vivacious and the center of much of the attention, particularly of the men. Emmet didn't come, however.

"I'm sorry Emmet couldn't be here, professor," Cleo told me as she entered through the gate in the fence between our properties—we were such a tight-knit community that, although we had wooden fences separating our gardens, each lot had a gate in the fence to each other lot it abutted. When I'd heard the squeak of the hinge of the gate between our two properties, I turned in anticipation. Cleo must have seen my face cloud up when she came through alone, as she was quick to apologize for Emmet's absence.

"He has a radio program to give today—actually a string of them. He's junior on the staff, so he draws the short straw on holiday coverage."

"I'm sorry he can't come," I said. I'm sure my voice made clear just how sorry I was. "Please let him know I'm sorry he couldn't come." I know I sounded idiotic, but I was just that disappointed.

The party went on famously, though, and I soldiered on. It was only later in the afternoon, when it was over, and the maid had cleared everything out and left me alone that it fully hit me. I was alone. I was really alone.

I felt sorry for myself. And when I felt truly sorry for myself, as I did now, I reached for the collections of English poets.

After nibbling on leftovers for dinner, I went out to the screened pavilion. It was a hot and muggy night. A typical July 4th evening in the lower middle South. Knowing it would be hot in the pavilion, I stripped down to gym shorts and sandals. I could have stayed in the air-conditioned house, but it was oppressive in the house in more ways than temperature and humidity. And oh so lonely. For the first time since Joanne and I had parted in Paris earlier in the spring I missed her—not sexually, of course, but for her companionship. For the sound of another voice. And maybe to help curb what was growing inside me. The desire that I had so carefully stifled.

Once in the pavilion, I realized I probably was out here to hear that voice of Cleo's that carried so well from her sun porch—and, more specifically, to hear another sex session between the two. Looking over the fence, though, I saw that her BMW convertible was gone. Emmet's Mustang was there, but Cleo had mentioned something about a dinner or some other affair she had to go to. Most likely he'd gone too—the Dutch colonial was dark.

I had come out with a bottle of Shiraz and a glass, and now settled myself in the loveseat glider at one end of the screened pavilion, and slowly buried myself in the poems of John Keats.

So engrossed had I become in the rhythm of the poetry that I wasn't immediately sure of the sound I heard—the sound

51

of the squeaky hinges of the gate in the fence between my property and Cleo's. Emmet was there, at the door of the screened pavilion, before I fully realized what was happening. And so strong had been the mystical worlds that Keats had been weaving in my mind that it didn't immediately register with me that Emmet was real.

He was naked, his manhood swinging low between his legs.

He pulled open the screened door to the pavilion and entered.

The whop, whop, whop of the overhead fan and the beating of my heart had become oppressive. I was close to hyperventilating. I couldn't bring myself to speak, still struggling to separate the Keats poems from reality. This couldn't be happening. I had so carefully sublimated these desires.

"Cleo told me that you wanted me to come," he said in that rich, low voice of his. "I've seen you watching me. I think I know what you want, what you need. I think you want me to come inside you. Tell me if I'm wrong."

He had moved to me, and I spread my legs to let him come into me very close. I could not speak. My answer was to reach out for him, my hand cupping his balls, lifting his jet-black, hardening cock with the heel of my hand, and leaning forward and opening my lips over the tan bulb of his ebony cock. My eyes locked on the thick blackness of the cylinder as, with a sigh, I pulled it, lovingly, inside my mouth cavity.

He fucked me in the glider, crouching over me, his hands under my buttocks, pulling them up to give his cock a deep angle. My wrists locked around his neck, my legs running up his torso, ankles on his heavily muscled shoulders. We kissed deeply, repeatedly, as he moved the glider back and forth, slowly, pulling my channel on and off his deeply buried staff.

I cried quietly while I told him how much this meant to me. I spoke of my first lover, a black field hand on my father's farm in Mississippi. Of our forbidden love—for more than one reason—in that time and place. How big and thick he'd been. How black his cock was. Nothing compared to Emmet, though. Thinner, not as beautiful. But my master all the same.

"Oh, god, how I'm loving this," I murmured. "How? How . . . did you . . .?"

"How did I know? The need was in your eyes. And you were there when I was fucking Cleo. Each time, it seemed. And I could see it in your eyes. You were having sex too, weren't you? With me?"

"Yes. Oh, god, yes. Like that. Oh, god, oh fuck. I'm going . . . to . . . coooome."

"I can come now too, if you wish. This is your wish? Do you want me to pull out and come?"

"Yes, come. But don't pull out. Silas, don't leave me. Give it to me. Big . . . black . . . cock." I moved my legs down and hooked my ankles together on the ledge of his bulbous buttocks, holding him fast to me, as his breath grew ragged and he jerked a couple of times—and bathed my insides.

We held there for several moments, neither one of us moving a muscle. "Silas. Was that the name of your first lover? Your black lover?"

"Yes."

"So was that part of your obvious fascination with me? Black cock?"

"Yes. I'm sorry, I know that sounds . . ."

"It's OK with me. I like white ass. Man, woman, it doesn't matter to me what white ass I'm fucking. It's all the same to me. So you like having this black cock deep inside you? Churning and revolving. Black cock is good enough for a university professor, is it? You like being mastered by a black man?"

"Yes, oh fuck yes," I cried out. He was working me again and I was panting hard. "Love that black cock," I whimpered. "you're my master. Black, black, black. Inside me. Deeper. Work me."

"Good to hear. You've got a sweet ass—for a professor. So tell me, professor. All of the lovers since that first one . . ."

"Black, yes. All black. That's what I want. He's got to be black. Oh, god, I want this so bad. Don't . . . talk . . . now. Just fuck."

He laughed a low, guttural laugh at that admission.

He worked me for a while, showing me he could do anything he wanted with me. And I melted to him. He slowed, though, not giving me another ejaculation just then. When we were cooling, he spoke again.

"What happened. Did you . . .?"

"I went to graduate school; he went to Iraq. He never came back."

"And after that?"

"Black. They all had to be black. And big . . . where . . . it counts. I know, that's so stereotypical. But I can't help it. It's got to be black and big. I've tried . . . but I can't."

We paused as a breeze went through the screening of the pavilion, setting the wind chimes to tinkling.

"The breeze feels good on my back," Emmet murmured.

"I'm sure it does. But you hardly raised a sweat. And it's so hot and humid tonight."

"Is this how Silas fucked you? Slow and easy?"

"He was usually very anxious. Impatient. Hard and fast."

"Would you like that now—for the memories?"

"Any way you want. But, oh, god, could you? Would you?"

He fucked me that second time with me bent over the table and holding the far edge with my fists for dear life as he crouched over me from behind and pounded me and pounded me and pounded me. This time after I'd ejaculated onto the floor of the pavilion under the table, he pulled out of me and shot up the small of my back. Then he thrust back inside me, laced his arms under my arm pits, locked his fists behind my neck, arched my back up to him, and fucked me hard until he came again.

"Silas do it like that?"

"Not nearly that well," I whimpered.

"You had enough?"

"Never enough."

"Would you like me to come inside with you? Sleep with you tonight?"

"Cleo?"

"Cleo was called away on business. We have three days and nights."

"Ah."

* * * *

Total surrender to my need.

Emmet was laying at the foot of my bed, the small of his back on the bed, his tan-soled feet on the floor, muscular legs spread. He was holding and waving his erect cock with one hand, and he had his head raised, looking past that, down the line of his luscious black torso, to where I was crawling along the floor toward him. All propriety and pretense out the window. Just the need and the desire. And that big, black cock.

"Black cock, black cock. Come and get it," he was singing in a rich, deep, quiet voice. He was grinning at me.

When I reached the bed between his spread legs, I went up on my knees and reached out with trembling hands and touched his cock on either side with the tips of my fingers. I ran my fingers up and down the sides of the staff, lovingly. I followed the line of the thick vein on the underside with my thumb. Looking down the line of his magnificent ebony torso at me, Emmet grinned and a deep, growly laugh bubbled up from deep inside him. His cock was getting bigger, harder under my worshipping touch.

I leaned in and gently rubbed the jet-black phallus on each of my cheeks, making soft mewing sounds, showing my pleasure, my awe.

"Suck my black balls, professor. Show me how much you want me—what you'll do for a black master, to have a big, black cock ruling you. This isn't about me. This is about you, what you need and want and have been denying yourself for too long."

I took each orb in turn in my mouth and then both of them together, separating and moving the nuts into my cheeks on each side. I hummed softly, vibrating the balls in my cheek cavity, and he arched his head back, staring at the ceiling, and gave me a low growl of a moan. I was holding his cock cupped in a hand, loving that it was still growing, still getting harder, throbbing.

"You do this for your black soldier boy?" he asked in a low, hoarse voice.

"Mmm, mmm," was the best I could manage.

"It's surely a mystery that he ever left you and went to war then. Are you my little white man whore, professor? My black cock your idol, your god?"

"Mmm, mmm."

"Lick it. Make what you love a lollipop."

After moving my mouth away from his body, pulling his balls taut and extending them, being rewarded by a deep groan from Emmet, I released his ball sack, ran my tongue up his shaft and slowly licked across and around the purple bulb of his cock, which twitched against the hand gently cupping it. I ran the other hand up his belly and smooth, hard, ebony chest and played with his nipples, one after the other with a thumb and forefinger.

"You want it inside you now, don't you? Down your throat, rubbing your tonsils, don't you, professor?"

"Yes," I whimpered. "Be good to me, Emmet. It's been so long. I need it so bad."

"Well, all right then. You can suck it now."

My mouth opened down over his cock. I shuddered with pleasure, desire . . . and surrender.

Minutes later I was straddling his hips, positioning his bulb at my hole, groaning in ecstasy as I slowly sank on my idol, what at this moment was my god. His hands on my waist, he grinned wide, murmuring that I was free, that it was all mine, that he knew this was what I needed, what I wanted beyond all else in life. Pulling it deep inside. Riding it, riding it hard. Black cock, black cock, black cock. BLACK COCK!

All those years of work, of self-denial. Jettisoned. Out the window. I . . . couldn't get . . . enough . . . of black cock.

* * * *

July and August were heaven. The first week in September I met Joanne in Paris and we went to Oxford for a week before coming home.

When we arrived home, the Dutch colonial next door was empty. No one could tell me where or why Cleo and Emmet had moved away. Everyone seemed pleased they were gone, though. Just too different. They didn't fit in.

I was devastated, of course. But everything was relative. I had had my summer of bliss and memories.

And Emmet had told me about the young hunk of a university assistant football coach down the block—and what he really wanted to do and that he'd confided to Emmet that I aroused him. And the coach was black too and was especially anxious to meet up with me when Emmet told him what I thought of and what I'd do for black cock.

Ernestine

I'm not sure why I went to Club 216 that night. I'd joined months before but had gone only rarely. Joining put me on their e-mail list, though, and I kept seeing announcements go by of their semiannual beauty contest. It didn't pay much attention to it—or at least I didn't think I had—but that Saturday night found me there, just a couple of table rows away from the stage. I was by myself at the table. I'd had some come by and give me the look, but I was lethargic and just let it ride. I think that was my problem at the time. I was lethargic about just about everything. Nothing was turning me on much. I needed some pizzazz in my life.

I'm not sure I went to the club on beauty contest night with any thought of adding pizzazz to my life. But maybe my subconscious was doing more work than I was. I do know that I was bored and out of sorts.

The contest was done in rounds, with the tamer contests coming earlier in the night. The one going on on stage when I arrived was an evening gown contest. Some of the dolls up there were real beauties who, I thought, could stand their own in a state pageant. All had great figures and good faces and looked terrific in the often highly suggestive gowns. That round went off really well with the audience too.

There was a packet of thick-papered cards on the table I sat at giving the names and numbers of the contestants in various rounds with boxes that patrons could tick off to vote their favorite. Half of the vote total came from the patrons who voted and half was done by a panel of three judges. It all was quite elaborate and well thought out, to my mind. An announcer repeated the names and numbers as the contestants strutted across the stage, each with a number pinned to a hip.

I hadn't planned on doing any voting, but the surprisingly high quality of what was up there swept me up into the spirit of the contest. I found myself looking and comparing. After each had walked across the stage alone and stopped at a mike and breathed their name into that and done what they could to sell their personality, all of them were brought out to stand in a cattle line for several minutes. This, I assumed, was to give the patrons a last chance to compare them and vote. That's when I did that—considered them as a group and started picking out my favorites.

It only took me a couple of moments to isolate my three favorites: Sandi Sweet, Ernestine Boudreau, and Linda Lays. At first I didn't realize that they all had something in common. Then I realized the ones I'd picked were all black. There was another black one in the contest, but a bit too much weight on the bones was what didn't sell me on that one. There were whites, Hispanics, blacks—and even a Filipino up there. So I thought for a moment about why I'd focused on the blacks. Maybe that was something I'd been missing. I never had considered color in my choices. Maybe it was blacks that attracted me and I hadn't even known that before.

The night was young and already it wasn't a loss to me. I got a little thrill out of considering blacks. Got a little of that pizzazz buzz. I'd meant to leave after that, not knowing if I could endure the talent round, but just that little buzz was enough to keep me there.

I scrutinized the contestants again and voted Ernestine Boudreau. That one had the best set, I thought. Like two ripe cantaloupes. And a good face too. Curvy thighs and a big butt.

60

The talent part wasn't much better than I thought it would be, but I endured. Nearly all sang and nearly all sounded alike. I didn't vote that round at all. They did it in their evening gowns.

The swim suit competition was a bit buzzier, and I concentrated on the three I'd picked out earlier. Once again the vote went to Ernestine Boudreau. Those melons and that big butt just couldn't be beat.

First thing I knew, it was midnight, and a good many of the patrons were gone. The lights were turned down, almost ceremoniously, at the stroke of midnight. I was ready to gather myself together and head on home when they announced that the next round was a wet T-shirt competition. What was left of the crowd put up a pretty noisy sign of appreciation with cat calls and pounding on the tables. With a thought to Ernestine's rack, I settled back into my chair.

As far as I was concerned Ernestine Boudreau won that one hands down. Ernestine came out in hot pink short shorts and black mesh stockings and spike heels. A slit up the sides of the shorts showed that the stockings were held up with a red garter belt. The white T-shirt, which had "Fuck You" emblazoned in pink across the front, was a couple of sizes too big, but once the bucket of water was slashed down Ernestine's front and over the shoulders, it clung so tight along the contestant's chest that the words got sucked right into the cleavage. Those hard, round melons just took my breath away. The nipples were huge, black through the opaque material of the wet T-shirt, with dusky aureoles the size of silver dollars.

One of my hands, almost too shaky to mark a box, went to the score card. The other one went to my lap. No lethargy in me now. I was pumped. And I could hardly wait to get home to do the pumping.

At the end of that round, the MC said to hold off on the voting, because the contestants were going to come out and do a walk-through in the audience. I about hyperventilated.

I really did think I was going to die on the spot when Ernestine Boudreau sat down at my table, right next to me, and gave me a really big smile.

"You all liked what you saw up there, honey? You give little ole Ernestine your votes?"

"Sure did," I answered, my voice thick as molasses so that I could hardly speak.

"I was watchin' you too, hon. You're a real looker. Haven't seen you in here before. I like what I see too."

"Um, I think they're calling the contestants back to the stage now."

And indeed the MC was calling them back, saying it would be a few minutes, but that the next and last round—the topless competition—was coming right up.

The topless competition. I practically melted. I moaned. But I didn't realize why I had moaned until it dawned on me that Ernestine had a hand underneath the surface of the table, resting on my groin and not exactly motionless.

"My, you is a big boy, ain't you? And enjoying this show, I can tell. This because of me?"

"Yes, I think so," I squeaked.

"And how about me? You like what you feel here?" A hand was guiding one of mine to between the thighs of those pink short shorts.

After a little involuntary yelp, I breathed a "Yes." This was almost too much for me to take, though. I couldn't take my eyes off the cleavage waving in front of my face.

"I . . . I think you're being called back to the stage," I mumbled. This had to stop or I'd shoot off right here.

"Fuck 'em, Sweetie. I think I got my prize right here. I think you're what I came for tonight."

I know I mumbled something then, I just never remember what. I'm sure it was brilliant, though, because Ernestine came up with an idea then. The hand went away from my crotch, though, which was both a blessing and a tragedy.

"You ever been to Boudreau's Books?"

"No, I haven't. Boudreau. Is that you?"

"Yep, that's me. I got my own bookstore. And I got books in the backroom that I bet you've never seen before."

"I'm sure," I answered. And I was sure, very sure. I'd never any thought about any of this before. I'd never imagined what a turn on it could be.

"How about we go to my bookstore for a little private reading."

"Now?" I burbled.

"Why sure. That would be what would make it a private reading. It's just three blocks from here."

I'm sure I answered something witty and worldly to that too, but it's a matter of lost history, whatever it was.

I remember being relieved it was pushing 1:00 a.m. and pitch dark for those three blocks, as Ernestine was hanging onto my arm like I might cut and run at any second and there'd been no change of clothes. The T-shirt was beginning to dry—but not enough not to draw the attention of any cop that was cruising by. Luckily, none did.

Ernestine was right. I hadn't seen anything like the books that were on the shelves in that back room of the bookstore. I hadn't even thought of anything like this going on—or that I'd find it a turn on. But I did.

I was standing, facing a bookshelf, and leafing through a book that had very explicit illustrations when Ernestine came around between me and the shelf, sank down in front of me, fiddled with my zipper, extracted my hard cock, and laughed a guttural laugh.

"Got me a big white boy, I do. All mine. Real sweet."

I groaned and sighed as ruby-red lips descended over my bulb and stopped there for me to feel the pressure and hear the sucking sound—and to release a deep moan—before the lips sank down my shaft and started a slow pumping rhythm.

After several moments in gloryland, I heard the breathy instruction cut through the fog. "Now me. Over on the desk."

The mouth was gone. After a minute of savoring the sensations I'd been awarded, I turned to find Ernestine already at the desk, that big butt resting on the edge; legs spread; stilettos flat on the floor, with well-turned ankles turned in; pink short shorts on the floor off to the side; heel of hands pressed into the desk top at either side of the slim hips; and giving me a saucy "Come hither" smile.

"On your knees. Taste what Ernestine's got for you."

I went down on my knees between the spread, black-mesh-stockinged thighs. I started with kissing the ebony brown flesh above the tops of the stockings, where the garters of the belt snapped on.

Ernestine groaned and gave a little sigh of appreciation. "Chocolate candy for my baby."

The bikini panties had a crotch slit in them and I reached in and pulled Ernestine's big, black cock out. I rubbed it, lovingly, on both cheeks and hummed low. That was the first time I realized that she had turned on sound somewhere, and there was a low-volumed, sensuous instrumental tune, with a steady beat, playing in the background. The lights had also been turned to a subtle bluish tint and were preprogrammed, I guessed, because they went through a cycle that would turn purplish and then, by the time we were finished, a virulent red.

As Ernestine obviously wanted me to do and enjoyed, I worshipped that cock before sliding it into my mouth. I'd sucked and fucked before, but never like this. Never with someone dressed as a woman—and a luscious one to boot. The thought of that made me rise from giving attention to that cock and bend over her as she arched her back and pulled the T-shirt off. My lips and teeth went to those firm, ripe melons, and I engorged on the fruit, as she sighed and growled and emitted deep rumbling noises from the gut.

Her voice was a rich baritone. The success with which she'd carried herself on stage had made that escape me, although, for the talent part, she'd sung a smoky song in a deep alto just like most of the other contestants had done.

I looked up. The wig had either been taken off or had fallen off. Ernestine's head was covered in short, black, kinked hair. The contrast with the dangling earrings, heavy eye shadow, and ruby-red lipstick was startling. But it was striking too. It gave me that buzz of something unexpected, something new and different, arousing. Highly arousing. Overpoweringly arousing.

I went back down on my knees, and slid as much of her cock inside my mouth as I could. I couldn't manage it all—and I had trained myself to this, to deep throating. But she was gigantic, and thick. And jet black. I shuddered at the thought of the blackness of her. I was trembling with lust, with want. I'd never known. Never known I could be turned on like this by a transvestite. Never known how I subconsciously lusted after a black cock.

"I wanna fuck you now," Ernestine said with a low growl. "You take black cock, don't you, baby?"

"Damn straight, I do," I answered in a growl.

"Oh, I can keep it straight until you come, doll."

It had taken an eternity—a glorious eternity—for me to sink down on the cock. Ernestine hadn't moved from being perched on the edge of the desk. She had made me open the condom packet and crown her first—her assurance, she said, that I knew what was happening and wanted it. At her instruction I had mounted her, facing her, my knees on the desk on either side of her hips. Her fists were locked behind the small of my back, and my torso was arched back over empty space. The edges of the fake gems in the gaudy rings on her fingers were cutting into my back, but I didn't care. All of my attention was elsewhere. I was relaxed everywhere but in my channel, which was strained, muscles undulating over the big, fat, buried black cock. All of my attention, sensations focused there. I hadn't thought it possible. But it was all inside me. Deep inside. I had all of her. Hard and throbbing. My arms were dangling, useless, at my side, my head was flopped back, my eyes counting the tiles in the ceiling, and then the dots inside the tiles, although I really wasn't thinking about anything but the cock working inside me.

My voice with a mind of its own, murmuring, "fuck, fuck, fuck, oh, god, fuck, fuck, fuck," in a low monotone.

"Fuck yourself on it now, littl' darlin'." The voice low, thick with want, a rich baritone. Commanding. It be obeyed.

Using my knees for leverage, I began to pump my channel up and down on the throbbing cock. Groaning, grunting, moaning, sighing. The music was getting louder, the beat heavier, the tempo faster. I fucked to the changes in the tempo. The lights were turning a hot red.

"Yes. You're so sweet. Sugar sweet. I'm goin' to the beach next week. Might take you with me."

"Yes," I hissed.

"My friends, Sandi Sweet and Linda Lays, they's taggin' along too. They's like sugar too. White sugar. You gonna let them fuck you too, sweetie?"

"Yes, oh god yes!" I cried out as we shot off together.

Loving Wife

"What's for dinner? Lamb chops, I hope. You do those so well."

"Of course, if that's what you want, Ely. If that's what you want, than that's what we'll have."

He's got no taste buds left, I think. What does he care if it's lamb, pork, or shit? Note to self—while I try to keep my voice from having the sarcastic edge Ely had complained about of late. Of course we don't have any lamb chops in the house. I'll have to go to the market.

"And grapefruit for breakfast, I hope."

"Yes, we have that."

"Pink grapefruit. You know I like that so much better."

"Sure, of course."

Trying to stay pleasant here. Now I'll have to go to the market for sure. The grapefruit we have isn't fuckin' pink. OK, control yourself, Kyle. You can make it out of the bedroom with this smile on your face. And don't even look in Wolfgang's direction. I know the prick has a self-satisfied sneer on his face.

Flung to the back of the panty. Pushed down on my knees. Tell me you don't want it, he says. Just say you don't. Fumbling with the zipper of his fly. Can't get to it fast enough. Licking down the side of it and then, with a sigh, opening my mouth over the bulb. Desperately wanting it to be hard, wanting him to fuck me. Now!

For better or for worse the minister had said in the ceremony. And I hadn't a single qualm about saying yes. I'd wanted Ely so desperately. I loved him desperately. I also wanted him inside me—constantly.

I still love him desperately. I don't want him to go. This is the absolute worst. And I . . . just . . . don't know if I can hang on. I had no idea how this would affect my needs. I don't know how I can hide my bitterness and my fear—and, worse, my physical wants—from him. There's nothing he can do about them anymore.

He's thirty years older than you are, everyone said. Don't get involved. You're barely twenty. You're just a student he's pulled out of his class. You know nothing about life yet. You haven't lived. He'll be sixty-five when you're thirty-five, and we all know how much—how often—you've got to have it. And whatever you do, don't marry the guy. He's vigorous now, yes. But at sixty-five?

Ely was good to me—very good. He could take care of me as often as I needed it. He kept in good shape and was active. I had no doubt that even at sixty-five he could give it to me. And sex wasn't everything. We had good times together. A hard cock was most things to me, of course, I won't deny that. But I loved—no, I love—Ely for so much else. Sex isn't it all. I keep telling myself that. And I do so want to believe it. It's Ely I wanted—who I want even now.

But who would have known that the question of sixty-five would be irrelevant? He wasn't going to make fifty-five even. Pancreatic cancer doesn't give you many options—or much time. And there's nothing pleasant about the time it does give you.

It hadn't been too bad for six months. I didn't have to work. We had plenty of money, and I could take care of him as long as he was still mobile. I'd had no idea I'd turn out to be a housewife taking care of an invalid—one old enough to be my parent. But it wasn't too bad for the first several months. We even still could fuck. He could maintain an erection and we both could get satisfaction with me riding the cock. He was still just about as big and as long-lasting as I could take.

But cancer takes its toll. And Ely wasn't going to be going into that good night easily. He railed at his sickness. He was demanding and bitter, especially at first. It taxed our relationship, of course.

Just leave him, my young friends would say. He can't expect you to stay and take care of him after he no longer can take care of your needs. It's not like you are a married couple.

Oh, but we are a married couple. We did the ceremony and everything. I know that's not supposed to mean as much between those of the same sex as between a man and a woman—especially ones with children—but it had meant even more to Ely and me. We were declaring a love and a commitment that would close doors to us and make people turn away. That ceremony had required so much of us.

And I still love him. I can forgive his moods and his demands. I know I would be so much worse if it was me dying from cancer like that—and painfully.

I just get so jittery and on edge myself. I have needs. I always did. I wouldn't have let him invite me to his home for special tutoring in the first place if I didn't know that he wanted to fuck me—that I wanted him to fuck me. I'd heard what he had and what he could do with it—and how much stamina he had. I needed that. I wanted that.

I fell in love with him, Professor Ely Silver, later. But I never fell out of love with his cocking.

I sure could use that now. But it was something he no longer could give. He was bitter enough about that for both of us. I needed to just grit my teeth and tough it out.

I was caught between a rock and a hard place when Wolfgang came to us. Ely had gotten to be too much for me to handle. He couldn't walk on his own—couldn't hardly move on his own. He was heavier than I was. I couldn't get him to the tub or even to the toilet and everything was getting out of hand.

He had to have a nurse. And he had to have one who could handle him.

Wolfgang was a big chunk of a man. Not fat; all muscle. Germanic. Organized, very capable . . . and demanding and knowing what the situation was—Ely and me living as a married couple—and how much he was needed to help with Ely. And, physically, Wolfgang could handle me as easily as he could handle Ely.

Oh, god. He's just upstairs. We can't let him hear us. Don't tease me. All of it. Deep. Hard. Oh shit. I want it so bad. My back chaffing against the brick fireplace wall at the back of the pantry as he pushes me up and down the bricks by the force of his cock, My knees clinging to his waist above his hip joints. Locking my ankles across the top of his bulbous buttocks. Gyrating my pelvis; fucking myself on his thick cock in frantic counterthrusts. Gotta have it. Gotta have it. Give it to me. GETITGETITGETIT! Wolfgang laughing deep in his throat. Thrusting harder, deeper.

I didn't look at Wolfgang as I backed out of the sick room. Just the one time. But I was walking on eggs. Ely couldn't know. The final thrust of the knife. I couldn't let Ely know how bad it was for me. It wasn't his fault. He felt bad enough that he couldn't give it to me. That he was leaving me so soon. It wasn't anything like we had planned. We had foreseen and planned for the thirty years of marriage thing, knowing that he probably would go first. We'd been so rational, so civilized, so reasonable about all that. We'd agreed that the sex drive would decrease for both of us over time—we'd mellow out together. Other couples with an age difference like this had told us it would be fine.

Well, his was gone. Mine was aching.

I couldn't let him know how much it mattered. The shattering of that dream. It was bad enough for him for what he faced. He couldn't know what it was doing to me.

Just months. Weeks even. Why couldn't I just hold on? But I didn't want to think about that. I didn't want him to go at all. I think he was accepting this better than I was now. Why couldn't I fuckin' just not want it so bad? And why was it putting me on such an edge? So close to lashing out whenever Ely makes a request I haven't anticipated. And Wolfgang there now, in the room, ready to move between us.

I couldn't let that happen. Not again. I couldn't let anyone come between me and my husband—certainly not in Wolfgang's way.

Trembling after we'd both come. You want it again, don't you? he asks, with a sneer in his voice. A randy little Kyle, ain't you? Tell me you don't want it again. How long since he's given it to you? Tell me this was a mistake, that you don't want it again, or we go again. I'm hard for you again. Whimpering, I don't answer. My instinct is to cut and stumble out of the pantry. To call the agency and have Wolfgang replaced immediately. Tonight. Instead I climb down off his hips and turn in his arms, facing the bricks of the fireplace wall. He laughs as I push my buttocks into his groin and reach back for his cock. You're such a slut, he mutters, as he slams back into me and I stuff a fist in my mouth so that my cries can't be heard upstairs. "Yes, yes, fuck me hard, I'm screaming in my mind. And he's doing just that—again."

I know he thought he was settled in to getting paid several ways, but it's been a week and I've avoided being alone with Wolfgang and haven't even given him more of a glance than I have too—even though his muscled body and that cock that I know so well now have me trembling knowing his eyes are following me around the room. Knowing. Waiting.

It was a relief, actually, to need lamb chops and pink grapefruit. I had to get out of the house. A trip to the market was what I needed to cut the tension—the tension of having to be cheery with Ely no matter what he was whining for and the tension of having Wolfgang follow me around the room with his eyes, rubbing his basket with a meaty fist where Ely couldn't see him from the bed.

I had a package of fresh lamb chops and a few other items in my basket and was standing in front of the grapefruit bin, trying to remember how you could tell which were the best ones—and laughing bitterly internally that I was being such a housewife about it. Ely couldn't taste much of anything anymore. If the grapefruit was just pink inside when I cut it, that would satisfy his want. If only all of his wants were that easy to satisfy. If only my own wants didn't need to be satisfied so badly.

I was squeezing the fruit too hard. This one was bruised. In my youth, I would have just tossed it back in the bin and picked out another. But Ely had told me to take responsibility for my actions—that even when there was no good solution, I should take responsibility for making one that did the least harm to others. A bruised grapefruit wouldn't do either a buyer or the store any good. I'd bruised it. I put the fruit in my basket and was picking out another one that I could serve Ely, when I looked up and caught him looking at me.

I was shocked. I hadn't seen Lloyd in years. Not since before I'd married Ely. He was from another world altogether. I shuddered at the thought of how easy it would have been for me to drift into that world. The leather world.

Lloyd was big and brawny, bold and brash and bald headed, but hairy everywhere else to make up for that. Covered in tattoos and body piercings. Older than I was, but not as much older as Ely was. I'd always gone for older men.

He'd come "that" close to having me once, and I'd come almost "that" close to letting him have me. But there was Ely, a sharp contrast to Lloyd. Offering so much more—including love and commitment.

Holding a second pink grapefruit in my hand, I watched him move toward me. It stopped on the other side of the bin. I nonsensically held the grapefruit up over the bin, between us. Keeping Ely between us.

"I've heard you're having a rough time. You and Ely."

"Times have been better than now, yes," I answered.

"It's good to see you Kyle. I think of you often."

I didn't say anything. I didn't want to say that I thought of him often too. I hadn't—for years. But since Ely went into the bed for the last time, I'll have to admit that I'd thought about Lloyd too.

"Really tough about Ely. It's been a slow going, I guess."

"Yes," I said. But I said it with a little bit of resentment. It wasn't too slow for me. Other than all that went with dying from pancreatic cancer, I hadn't wanted my time with Ely to be a second shorter than it had been.

"Can't fuck with that sort of thing, is what I've heard."

I didn't respond. After looking around to see if there were any other store patrons within earshot, which, thankfully, there weren't, I picked up another grapefruit and held it with the other one in front of me, between me and Lloyd. As a reminder of who was there even though he wasn't there.

"I could help with that," Lloyd continued. "Ely need never know, if that's what you want. I didn't think you'd last with him a week. But you've done good. And I bet you've done good by him. All that time I was tryin' to get you, though, I could see that you couldn't go long without it."

"I . . . I need to get back to the house," I muttered. "Good seeing you, though, Lloyd. And thanks, but . . . well, I think I need to go back. I can't be away too long."

"I'll be outside—in my truck—if you . . . you know."

And then he was gone. If I'd expected him to be pushy, it was my surprise. I found I was trembling. Had I wanted him to be pushy?

"Excuse me? Are you about done squizzin' them grapefruit?"

I snapped out of my trance. An elderly lady was trying to get to the grapefruit bin.

"Oh, sorry," I said. "Yes, I'm done. Yes, indeed, I'm done." I was so tired. I was past done.

I put the two good grapefruit back into the bin. Then I walked around the grocery store—in a trance—putting items from my basket back where I'd gotten them. All but the bruised grapefruit.

Responsibility. Ely had taught me to take responsibility. He'd also taught me to problem solve. He'd been the best damn math professor in the university. Everyone wanted to take his courses. And he probably had been the best cocksman in the university too. All of the young men who went for that sort of thing wanted to be bedded by him. But he had picked me.

Ten minutes after I'd entered his house for the special tutoring I hadn't really needed, he was doggie fucking me on the carpet in his living room. And I couldn't get enough of his cock. Or of him. I was in seventh heaven when he wanted me to move in with him—and had risen to ninth heaven when he said he wanted me to marry him—to forever and ever with him.

But he'd also taught me to problem solve. To make whatever compromises had to be made to get to a "best-case" goal. To take responsibility for paying for fruit I'd bruised.

"You sure you want this, sir?" the checkout clerk enquired in a polite voice. "The fruit looks like it's been bruised."

"Yes, I like it that way, thanks. Just ring it up, please. I'm in a bit of a hurry."

Lloyd had waited. He was leaning up against the fender of his double-cab metallic black-painted truck and looking confident and a bit amused as I exited the grocery store with the one grapefruit in a plastic bag.

He drove me to his farm a couple of miles out of town and parked behind his barn. We fucked first in the backseat of the cab. After I'd sucked him big to the sound and feel of his thick cock ring clicking against my teeth, he pulled me up and screwed my channel down on his cock, with me facing him, and the soles of my feet leveraging off the back window of the cabin on either side of his head. Just watching the tattooing on his chest, arms, and torso undulating and feeling his nipple rings cold on my tongue made me come quickly inside his pumping fist. He laughed and kept on with his own rhythm of the fuck to a long, hard, glorious ending.

I couldn't stop moaning and "oh shit yessing" when he'd gone quiet.

"Been a while since you had it good, hasn't it?"

I said nothing, because I couldn't lie. Wolfgang had been good too. But it had been a week. Wolfgang was so right. I was a slut. It was a problem. But it was one to be compromised. I knew that now. I knew what Ely would want me to do. He wouldn't want to know, of course. But I knew it was what he would want. It would make me a hell of a lot easier to live—and to approach dying—with.

Lloyd said he wanted to fuck me properly, in the house, in his bed. But we only made it just outside the truck door. He looked at me, standing there, nude, hard, trembling, wanting him again. Now. And he pushed me down on the small of my back

74

on the passenger seat. I raised one foot to the corner of the windshield inside and the other to the door frame on the other side of the passenger door, and he stood on the running board, crouched over me and worried my nipples with his teeth as his piercings jangled and his tattoos moved in waves and his cock thrust and thrust and thrust, punishing my prostate ecstatically with that thick cock ring.

"The house," he murmured when we'd both come.

"I can't. I do have to get back. And I've got to go back to the grocery store."

"How often do you go to the grocery store?"

"Usually every Thursday."

"Do you think you can make it on Tuesdays too?"

"Uh, I don't know."

"Don't go shittin' me now. I think I know you pretty good. You need it more than once a week. Might as well be in for a penny as well as a pound. Like I said. Nobody needs to know. Not Ely or anyone else. I've wanted you ever since I didn't get you."

A penny and a pound. I laughed. This is one reason I liked older men. They used such strange expressions. Such apt ones too, though. This one gave me comfort. Deciding to do it was one thing. Feeling brave enough to do it as much as I needed it was another thing. For some strange reason my thoughts went to Wolfgang. God, he'd had a powerful thrust with that thick cock.

I picked a different checkout clerk when I went back to the grocery store for lamb chops and another pink grapefruit— I'd left the bruised one in Lloyd's truck, along with those intentions I couldn't live up to as well as all of the inhibitions I'd left home with.

Outside of the grocery store I made a cell phone call from the car.

"Ms. Taylor? This is Kyle Silver. You may remember, we talked about that double room at the nursing home, where my husband, Ely, could have a full-care room for the remainder of his needs and I could have the room next to him so I could be there full time too. If it's still available, could we occupy as soon as possible? It's vacant now, still? Can we arrange transportation tomorrow?"

When I entered the house, I put everything away in the kitchen except the grapefruit. I dug out the recipe for lamb chops that Ely liked the best. Then, taking the grapefruit, I climbed the stairs to Ely's bedroom. I stood at the door for a few moments, composing myself, and calling up my cheeriest smile.

I entered the room. Ely was awake, grimacing in pain, but he put on a brave smile when he saw me. Wolfgang was dozing in the corner, but he snapped awaked when I entered as well.

"I got the grapefruit," I said. "A nice elderly lady helped me pick out the best one. You can have that and anything else you want for breakfast. And I think I'll bring a tray up and eat with you in the morning." I kept my voice upbeat, my smile my best.

"You're so good to me," Ely said.

"You are all the world to me, Ely," I answered. "We're going to make every minute count."

I looked over straight into Wolfgang's eyes. He was giving me a sneery, possessive smile of his own. I smiled back.

I'd give Wolfgang's thick cock the best ride of his life tonight. He'd get a good-bye bonus he'd never forget. And I wouldn't care if I did need the cock more than he needed my ass. I'd come to terms with that. I'd make Ely's last days the best that they could be. Every minute would be a testament of my love for him and how he could most comfortably conclude his days. And I'd do it without tensions and bitternesses of my own. I'd found a way to take care of that.

Chaz's Choice

"Are you sure? You don't have to go through with this."

But, who was I kidding. Julio's choices had been shut down that first night—the night I'd found him supposedly by chance, but with chance having nothing to do about it. He'd been had even before I approached him at the Noobai Café, the discreet little gay hookup bar in the Restele district of Lisbon, not far from the Cuban consulate.

"I've done what you told me to do, Frank," Julio said. He was looking as much like the innocent and the deer in the headlights here on the street in Restauradores Square at the Pirata open-air café as he had that first night when he realized I was going to fuck him. "I have it all on a couple of CDs. It's in the hotel room you said I should book across the street."

I looked up at the façade of the Hotel VIP Executive Suite Eden as Julio gestured across the street. As I did so, I noticed two pair of eyes at a nearby table involuntarily follow Julio's gesture and my line of sight. Ours or theirs? They could be almost anything. American, Canadian, Cuban, Russian even. Not Chinese, though. Thank god for little favors. The Chinese were all over Lisbon with their ferreting. It was a gold mine. They understood that better than most.

I had a brief vision of nervous, luscious little Julio, all delicate beauty and noticeably dark skin, flashing dark eyes, and that curly black hair cascading around his face, standing at the desk of that expensive hotel and making reservations. I should have told him to check into a fleabag. So much of this had gone wrong. And so much was my fault.

"Get him to bring it to a hotel room, not the apartment," Peter, my handler, had said. "The safe house will not do for this. Meeting at a nearby café and casing it beforehand would be the best. You can have drinks—iced coffee or something—ordered from there to take up to the room."

That's when Peter had told me why we should have a drink—something that would cover the taste.

"Is that necessary, Peter?" I'd asked, shocked that it was coming to this. "He's just an innocent young man. Raw at the job. Isn't it enough that the Cubans will find him out?"

"You're our asset, Chaz," Peter had said—the name I'd given Julio of course not being my real name. Chaz wasn't my real name either, for that matter, any more than Peter was the name of the man giving me these horrifying instructions. "You're the one we must protect. You're a Canadian importer of Portuguese Vinho Verde wine here, making excellent local contacts. You are too valuable to us in this role. He must not be able to identify you."

"But he's barely grown," I said again—nonsensically, as I knew that wouldn't do a bit of good. But it meant something to me. It meant a whole lot to me. I'd never felt this way before in doing the job I had to do.

He'd been so shy and vulnerable—and, yes, I had to admit it, desirable—when I had pulled in beside him at the bar that first time. He obviously had only now worked up the courage to come to a gay bar, starved for the attention he needed and frightened silly by the risk he was taking, by the choice he was making just by being there.

It had taken three drinks to calm him enough that I could put my hand on his thigh and lean over and whisper into his ear what I could do for him. He trembled and his nostrils were flaring like that of a skittish thoroughbred race horse.

He had cried quietly when I covered his body and fucked him on the bed in the safe house apartment. I lay fully sheltering him under my body, as he shuddered and writhed. I kissed him in the hollow of his neck and whispered to him how wonderful his body was and how much it meant to me that he'd given himself to me, as I let my fingers stroke his scalp through his luxurious black curls.

He had been fucked before—years before he had entered the Cuban foreign service as a lowly code clerk—but it obviously had all been furtive and by young men who were no more experienced than he was. I was his first real man, the first man who knew how to work his body, how to give and take suck, what nipple play could arouse, how to play his channel with the cock.

"It is his inexperience and vulnerability—and the very reason that he is a lowly code clerk on his first assignment—that we chose him," Peter had told me. "These third world countries will never learn. They give the least training and preparation to the employees who have the greatest access to their secrets—the clerks who send and receive their communications."

"But is it worth it?" I'd asked.

Peter had looked sharply at me then. "You are not falling for the young man, are you?"

"No, of course not," I lied. "I just don't know what three months worth of cable exchanges between Havana and a small consulate in Lisbon can be worth."

"The Cuban Foreign Ministry loves to pontificate—and to share their wisdom with every embassy and consulate in their system," Peter answered. "There is something going on between the Castro brothers. We're sure that traffic will help us find out what that is."

It was only near the end of the third visit to the safe house, while I was sitting in the overstuffed armchair and, facing me, Julio was rising and falling on my cock with the strength of his knees on the arms of the chair and I was driving his cock like the gearshift of a sports car, that I told him what he could do for me if he wanted our encounters to continue.

The second and third times I'd made him contact me and beg for the meeting. I knew after the blow job I gave him in the second meeting that he was mine. But, as Peter had instructed me to do, I waited for him to ask me what he needed to do to keep me after I told him that it might be best, safer for us both, if we broke it off.

It was like shooting fish in a barrel. That had been Peter's observation, and then he'd laughed. I couldn't deny that the observation was apt, but I didn't laugh. I was too busy trying to hide from Peter that I had feelings for Julio now. That wasn't in the scheme at all; that quite purposely wasn't in my job description.

"I think we can go on up to the hotel room now," I said there at the table in the Pirata Café. "I was going to suggest that we take iced coffees up, but I see that you already have one. Do you want it refreshed?"

"No. No, thanks. I prefer it when it has gone lukewarm. I'll take this one."

"I'll order one then and we'll go up. Again, are you sure?"

I reached over and laid a hand on his thigh. He didn't flinch. We were way beyond that. He looked at me with trusting, desired-filled eyes. I hated myself at that moment.

We fucked languidly on the bed in the luxurious hotel suite, me taking him deep in a side split and arching his torso back to me so that he could turn his face and we could kiss deeply, me fucking his tonsils as much with my tongue as I was worrying his prostate with the bulb of my cock and him gasping and moaning. If it was a last fuck, I wanted it to be a memorable one—for me, even if it could not be for him. This time the tears were in my eyes.

He was dozing on the bed. The briefcase was propped up at the side of the desk I was standing beside while I looked out of the window down into Restauradores Square into the Pirata Café. I was fingering the two capsules in the pocket of the hotel robe I had pulled around my shoulders. I could just take the briefcase and leave now. I didn't have to go through with this. Peter would just have to live with half a victory. I could even just insist on being pulled out of Portugal.

80

I was such a fool, though. I knew that. I knew Peter—or whoever he really was. He wouldn't let it rest if I failed to use the capsules.

I felt my blood run cold as I looked down at the café and focused on what I was looking at. Those two men, those same two men who had involuntarily looked up when Julio pointed to the hotel from the café earlier. They were still there, in the café. And they were looking up at the window—at me. "He wouldn't let it rest," I muttered.

"What did you say?"

I turned toward the bed. Julio was sitting up and reaching for the cup of iced coffee he'd brought up from the café.

"Wait, Julio," I said. "Were you ever out of sight of that drink when you were in the café?"

"Well, maybe . . ."

"Stop! Don't drink that. Put it down. Come, out of bed and dress. We'll need to find a back entrance to the hotel."

"I don't understand."

"You don't have to understand, Julio. You just need to do it. Here. Give me that cup." I strode over and took it out of his hand. I also picked up the cup I'd brought upstairs. When I returned from dumping the liquid from those and the two capsules from my robe pocket in the commode, he was dressing as I had directed. Prepared to do anything I asked.

"What . . . ?"

"I don't know, Julio. I'll figure it out later. But we'll leave the briefcase here. That should mollify them for a bit. I just know we have to get out of this. Both of us."

The Negotiator

I wondered what he could tell about me that no one at home or the office—at least I hoped and always had thought—knew. He had introduced himself as Hal when he'd appeared beside me in Business Class and I'd stood from my aisle seat so that he could get over to the window. He'd had a friendly smile, and if I hadn't been busy during the first two hours over the Atlantic from New York going over the papers for my discussion in Birmingham at Smythe and Withers the next day, I'm sure that he would have wanted to chat.

I didn't like to work on business matters while I was flying, but there were hundreds of millions of dollars at stake in this bid we were making for providing a revolutionary model of catalytic converters to the British automobile manufacturers. Smythe and Withers were the manufacturer's agents, and my company was bidding against a French firm with a design of its own. We were well versed in the automobile industry, but almost nothing had been able to be gleaned about Smythe and Withers. I was my company's premier negotiator, but I didn't like to go into talks knowing so little about those I was negotiating with. As soon as I could use my laptop, I got busy trying to pull something more up from the Internet on that firm than I already had.

It was a frustrating hour and a half, and I perhaps had at least one more drink from the accommodating stewardesses and stewards than I normally would have if I wasn't distracted. Finding nothing new, though, I sighed with frustration and closed my laptop with a click.

"Working on an important presentation?" I looked over to the window seat. I had lost all realization that there was someone else there.

"Yes. One that's both important and frustrating," I answered. For the first time I focused on him. He was a few years older than I was and considerably better put together. We hadn't exchanged much in the way of a conversation, but he had one of those upper-crust British accents that companies like mine liked to have their chief operating officers to have to fool their stockholders into thinking they knew what they were doing. He was debonair, perfectly groomed, and designer dressed. His face was tanned and Hollywood-star chiseled, with those distinguished, precisely trimmed gray sideburns that spelled casual wealth and near-effortless success at anything he endeavored to do. He certainly seemed to exude self-confidence.

And there was that big smile he gave me whenever I looked his way.

Almost as a flood of revelation, three awarenesses hit me at once that took me away from business, which only served to show how focused I'd been before in finding out whatever else I could about this Smythe and Withers firm. But I could afford a side diversion now; there wasn't anything else I could do up here at altitude. I knew everything that was needed to know about the French firm, and I felt good about their end of the negotiations. They always sent the pompous ass, Jean Claude Dupre, to such bidding wars—and he always seemed to screw up his presentations and upset the very people he was pitching. I wondered what sort of power he had in that company not to have been shunted aside already—although, since "Dupre" was in the company title, I could guess at his leverage.

The first awareness was that increasingly my drinks were being delivered by a flouncy steward with dark eyes and hair flopping disingenuously over one eyebrow. The other one had a silver ring in it. But when he was serving me, all of his attention was planted on my seatmate, Hal, who rewarded him with the same warm smile I was getting.

The second revelation came as I followed the steward's gaze over to Hal's lowered seat tray, where the steward was placing a fresh martini and taking an empty martini glass away. There were two other objects on the tray that almost took my breath away—and seemed to be what was twitter-pating the steward as well. One was a paperback novel, with a familiar screaming title on the cover in gray and scarlet letters. I'm sure that most people had no idea what was inside the covers of John Rechy's *City of the Night*, but I had every reason to believe that it was a classic—and explicit—gay novel. And my seatmate, Hal, had it sitting out in plain sight.

And not only that. He also had a foil condom packet sitting there and was fondling it—that's the only appropriate verb I could use for the play of his long, sensuous, manicured fingers as they played with the packet.

It was obvious that Hal was projecting a clear message. I assumed it was for the steward, who was almost beside himself with interest, but, when Hal turned his smile on me and when I noticed that his thigh was right up against mine when there was more than enough room for us to be separated in our seats, I couldn't be sure.

And the reason I couldn't be sure was that Hal was just the sort of man I melted to. But secretly. It was something I'd never shared with either my family or my company. I led the perfect trophy blonde wife and two preciously beautiful children wealthy suburban life. And my company was perhaps one of the most conservative in the United States when it came to anything close to gender bending.

But I was instantly interested in Hal—perhaps even more than the steward who was virtually drooling over him was. What I found shocking was that Hal seemed to know that I was. I wondered, almost in panic, what had given me away.

But when Hal climbed—none too quickly—over me when the plane's interior lights had been dimmed and people had gone quiet and spoke in hushed tones to the steward in the aisle and both disappeared for nearly a half hour, I worked hard at convincing myself that it wasn't me that Hal had set his net for, but the steward. This impression was helped along when I noted that the condom packet no longer was on Hal's tray and didn't resurface for the rest of the flight.

The swishy steward's back pressed against the wall over the toilet in the confining Business Class toilet, his bare knees pressed into Hal's chest and his head bent forward by the curve of the plane's fuselage. His tongue is hanging out and he's making little yip, yip sounds as Hal, expensive trousers and briefs around his ankles holds the little bleach blond against the wall and thrusts a manly cock up into a tight hole. Again and again and again. A side-angle camera angle that shouldn't have been possible in the space showing the long, ribbed-condomed cock pulling nearly all the way out and then slamming home again. Repeating. The blond steward shuddering with each thrust. The camera focuses to the floor at Hal's feet, picking out the torn, now-empty, condom packet. Welcome to the mile-high club.

I shook my head, realizing that I had dozed off, if only momentarily, in a reverie. It had been long enough, however, for me to go hard. When Hall returned, his zipper was at half staff and his shirt wasn't tucked in as neatly as it had been when he'd left.

In Birmingham, as I struggled, half groggy from the effects of the trans-Atlantic flight, out to the taxi queue, I was completely disarmed and flummoxed when the rear passenger door to a black limousine opened in front of me, Hal leaned out of the door, and I heard him say, in a rich baritone, "Shall I give you a lift to your hotel room, then?"

* * * *

Hal proved to be an expert lover. He seemed to understand instinctively what I wanted—to be dominated and driven hard, but expertly. He took the initiative in everything, which was exactly how I liked to have my sex with men.

It started in the back of his limousine. As soon as my luggage was stowed in the trunk and I'd entered the back of the car, Hal pulled me close to him. He called out for his driver to take the long route to the hotel I identified as the one I was booked in, the Radisson Blu Hotel, and only then turned toward me.

"You don't mind that we take the long way, do you?"

"No," I said, breathlessly, hoping that this meant what I was taking it to mean.

"And you understand why I offered you the ride?"

"Yes," I answered in a tight voice.

"Which means I'm going to fuck you. I've wanted to do that all across the Atlantic."

It wasn't a question. He already had an arm around me and the other hand working my belt buckle.

"Yes," I managed to croak.

He didn't bother to do more than unzip himself and I was squatting in front of him and sucking his meaty cock erect. I just flipped the split foil condom wrapper on the floor of the car—with a vision of the one I'd imagined on the floor of the airplane toilet—after I'd rolled the disc down over his cock. Then, jacket, trousers, and briefs off, shirt unbuttoned, and tie being used as reins as Hal wished, I rode his cock. I first faced him, with the two of us kissing and him working my nipples with his mouth. Then I faced the front seat with him arching my torso back to him by pulling on my reversed tie and his other hand snaking around and milking my cock.

A second opened condom packet lay next to the first on the limo's rear seat floor. A spent condom, thick as a slug with the cum inside it, lay between the packets.

In the hotel room, after we had both taken a quick shower, him first, he took me again, hard, doggy style on the carpet before we'd reached the bed. We were both naked this time. His body was magnificent for his age. His cocksmanship—stroking vigor, staying power, and reload ability—was superb. Triple A in all departments. And a hunk on top of all of that. He brought a briefcase up with him, which he placed on the desk by the bed and opened to reveal a pile of condom packets, tubes of lubricant, and various toys, including a plow belt.

"From your responses in the car, I think you know what this is for," he said.

I didn't answer. I well knew what a plow belt was for. I had started to tremble in anticipation the moment he'd taken it out of the briefcase. He whipped the strip of black leather with hand holds at each end over my head, upending me on my belly, and proved that he could support my whole weight with his hand grips on the handles of the plow belt as he thrust his cock into me from the read and moved my channel on his cock.

He played me like a rag doll, totally dominating me, giving me exactly what I loved from a man.

I had no idea how he knew I'd let him fuck me let alone what I wanted in a fuck partner—but the experience was just too glorious for me to question. I probably should have questioned more, been more cautious in acquiescing to what he wanted to take from me, to give to me.

I slept, exhausted, after he'd pounded my ass for a third time on the bed. And when I woke, he was gone. There were no notes or any other indication of who he was or where he was. I doubted then that his name even was Hal. But that was OK. I'd been fucked well—and all of the tension of the coming negotiations for the catalytic converter bid had melted away.

Well, most of it.

* * * *

I wasn't picked up for the meeting at Smythe and Withers until the next, Friday, afternoon, which was meant to provide me sleep time. But its only real effect was to give me time to sharpen my nerves again over the coming meeting. I just wasn't used to knowing so little about those I was negotiating with. I had found references to the firm, and they did have a Web site, but they obviously were one of those old staid British firms that hid behind the doors of their exclusive gentlemen clubs. At least that gave me the clue that I'd best dress and act ultraconservatively.

I wondered what they would think if they knew that I'd let a stranger I'd barely met on an airplane into my hotel room to fuck my lights out with a plow belt immediately upon arrival in Birmingham. I almost was reduced to nervous giggles by that thought.

A vintage black Rolls Royce sedan with a stern-looking uniformed chauffeur met me at the hotel door to whisk me away to what proved to be not more than a four-block ride into a garage under a modern steel and glass high-rise building. It wasn't at all what I expected the building would be like that housed the Smythe and Withers offices.

The chauffeur parked in a remote, barely lit recess of the garage and waved me toward the distant elevator doors with the comment that I could find the offices I was looking for on the thirty-third floor. I wondered if it was a Britisher's way of putting an upstart American in his place by not letting me off at the elevator doors, but I was too preoccupied with the order of my presentation to take umbrage.

I almost was too preoccupied to notice the tableau I passed en route to the elevator doors.

If the ceiling light hadn't been on in the interior of the sleek forest-green Jaguar I was passing, I probably wouldn't have looked over at the automobile. And if I hadn't looked over there, I would have missed why the interior light was on. The passenger door was open, and with slight difficulty I discerned a pair of bare, pale legs, ending on argyle socks and tan loafers with tassels waving in the air, trying to find purchase on the door frame or to wrap themselves over the shoulders of the man who was hunched between them, fully suited in a black and gray silk pinstriped suit—obviously very expensively cut—and obviously fucking the young man lying on the small of his back across the bucket seat. The receiver's white knuckled fists were scrabbling at the upper reaches of the door frame, evidently attempting to keep his back from being bruised by the gear shift between the seats.

The bottom was being very vocal. But not in English. It sounded like French to me.

I lingered momentarily, watching, my mind connecting this taking with what I had gloriously experienced the previous evening and wishing that it was me being fucked. I liked everything that was assailing my senses with this encounter—the passionate cries of the bottom, the richness of both the automobile and the suit-clad taker, even the element of danger in the public nature of the sexual act and the incongruity of the dark garage and the lit Jaguar interior.

It was with a heavy sigh that I turned and walked toward the elevator doors. When I heard the cry of the bottom that he was coming, ejaculated in language that even I could understand, I turned and saw the man fucking the bottom tense and then fall on top of the other man, who hugged his assailants back closely with his bare legs, the tassels of his shoes swaying in air.

Again, as I waited for the elevator doors to hiss open, I wished that it had been me on the small of my back in the Jaguar. What I'd experienced when I arrived in Birmingham was still making me horny. In fact, with the difficult negotiations imminently facing me, I wished I was anywhere else, doing anything else.

I was kept cooling my heels in a mahogany-paneled reception room that could have come out of a seventeenth-century English castle for nearly an hour and then for twenty more minutes in a conference room with floor-to-ceiling glass windows overlooking downtown Birmingham after I had been introduced to a clutch of sour-looking old goats, as conservatively dressed as I had imagined, at the other end of the table from where I had been told to sit. I didn't remember all of the names, but I made sure that I latched into the two oldest goats of the lot, Robert Smythe and Halston Withers, who obviously were owners of the name on the door.

Neither one of the patriarchs seemed pleased at the delay. But it wasn't my delay. We obviously were waiting for something else to happen.

And then it happened.

The first "happening" was the appearance, wearing a silk black and gray pinstriped suit that was expensively cut but perhaps a bit rumpled today, of the Hal of my airplane flight followed by my dance on the clouds. I went numb but not numb enough not to catch him being introduced as Halston Withers Junior, who, to my terror, was going to handle the project contract negotiations for Smythe and Withers.

The second "happening" descended as Hal was apologizing for being late because he had been late in gathering up the negotiator for the French firm, Sean Dupre, who entered the conference room in Hal's wake. This quite obviously was not the sloven Jean Claude Dupre I had faced—and easily bested—in negotiations before. It was his very young, willowy, and handsome, in a sultry, Lord Byronish way, son, Sean. My eyes went automatically to his feet and my greatest fears were realized when I saw the tan tasseled loafers with the argyle socks peeking out below his trousers hem.

The greatest consternation of all was that Hal didn't even flutter an eyelash when he was introduced to me. He had known who I was all along.

My fears were confirmed after the two presentations were taken and hard questions asked of both but no indication was given of which one they favored. Darkness had already fallen on the city of Birmingham and the night lights had flickered on when Hal declared that we would resume discussions on Monday—that he was off to his country home for the weekend and, most alarming of all, that he was taking Sean Dupre with him.

I was half-heartedly invited to weekend with one of the junior partners, but he seemed relieved when I said I really should spend the time consulting with my company on the answers to some of the questions the negotiating firm had shot at me.

"May I see you for a moment before you leave," Hal Withers Junior said to me as the others were jacking themselves out of their chairs to the tune of more than one letting gas and milling about waiting for the session to dissolve.

I didn't know what to expect when Hal took me to his office. What I wanted was for him to lay me on his desk and fuck me to ecstasy. But that's not what happened.

"I personally find your proposal the better of the two—although neither is acceptable yet," Hal told me when we were alone.

"Hal . . ." I started to say, wanting to talk about something else entirely.

"Over the weekend I'd like you to reconsider all of your figures, Doug," he continued, very businesslike.

"It's a fair offer, Hal," I said. "Better than the French one if you look at the whole package."

91

He wasn't looking at me. He was fanning photographs out on the top of his desk. My heart nearly stopped when I leaned over and looked at them. They were of Hal and me doing our sexual exercises in my hotel room the previous night. The briefcase. The one he'd put on the desk. It had had a camera in it.

"I understand you work for a very conservative firm," Hal was saying, although I was too numb to pay too much attention to what he was saying. "And you have a lovely family—two children, I'm told."

That was like a dagger slipped between my ribs.

"You knew who I was on the plane, didn't you? And you meant for me to see what happened down in the garage, didn't you?" I asked in a strangled voice.

"But of course. That's what good negotiators do—scope out and use their counterpart's vulnerabilities. Luckily for you, Doug, the negotiations are still open. I am still working on Sean Dupre's vulnerabilities."

I wanted him to say more—to say something that validated our time together. But when he did speak again, he was still focused on the negotiations.

"Monday morning, Doug. I think you can come up with a lot better deal by then."

And then he was gone.

* * * *

What stung the most was not Hal's failure to tell me that I was the best he'd ever had in the sack—or even that he had targeted me for sex. It was a fetish of mine to be dominated by a tinge of cruelty. No, what hurt the most was his suggestion that I was an inferior negotiator. I was the pride of my company in negotiations.

I would not take this laying down, I thought. But then I laughed. I certainly so far had taken it laying down—with my legs open and begging for it.

When I got back to the hotel, I ordered dinner in and got right to work on the computer. I even called the research unit in the company back in New York, which was five hours behind the time in Birmingham, in early for their day. Where a barrier against information had been erected around the firm of Smythe and Withers, Robert Smythe and Withers, father and son, were people and may not be as well cordoned off as their firm. Hal had been right about vulnerabilities. I needed to know theirs.

In the end, Hal's base vulnerability was the same as mine. He had a wife who was quite active in charity events and children—ones both by the current wife and by a former one. And there was no hint in the public record of Hal Junior fucking men.

The public record also told me where Hal Junior's country home was—in the Cotswolds, a two-hour drive south of Birmingham.

Because I wasn't used to driving on the left and had trouble figuring out the road signs, it took me nearly three hours the next morning to reach his country house. The first people I encountered when I pulled into the forecourt of a rambling English Tudor residence were a young couple looking to be in their early twenties who were decked out in tennis togs and who were swinging tennis rackets. They introduced themselves as Halston Wither's older children, Victoria and Edwin—Vicki and Eddie—and I introduced myself, daringly, as an American business acquaintance of their father's who their father had invited down for the weekend.

I hoped not only that I was bearding Hal in his lair sufficiently to keep him from declaring I hadn't been invited and sending me off in embarrassment but also that the house had sufficient bedrooms to make it believable that I had been invited. From the size of the edifice that I could see, though, that wasn't likely to be a problem. It could as well be a country hotel as a country house.

At the bottom of the briefcase I was carrying up to the front door of the small castle were the photographs Hal hadn't taken with him when he left me in his office the previous evening—but that I had had the presence of mind to snarf up. Those photographs could be used both ways, especially now that I knew that Hal had a wife and children just as I had.

"Jolly good," Eddie said. "Daddy is off on a shoot with that Frenchie he dragged home for the weekend. Won't he be surprised when he finds you already settled in when he gets back?"

"I haven't the slightest doubt about that," I answered.

"You're just in time for tea," Vicki said. "Eddie can show you to a bedroom and then you two can join Mam and me in the conservatory."

It was a piece of cake—or biscuit, I guess, in the British lingo. There I was, sitting all smiles between the newer Mrs. Withers and daughter Vicki, with son Eddie across the tea table from me and with a third cup of tea in my hand, when Hal entered the conservatory all abluster with what he termed to be a splendid shooting day. He was so well tailored that he looked like he'd just walked off a movie set rather than a slog through forest and marsh. He said that Sean Dupre was all in from the day's sport and had already gone to his room.

As I was sitting where I could see the grand staircase in the foyer and had seen Hal and Sean enter the house and mount the stairs a good thirty minutes earlier, I had a fair idea what Sean Dupre was tired from and what else other than stairs Hal had been mounting.

I had to hand it to him. Hal acted exactly like he really had invited me. Only a wry smile on his lips revealed to me—and I trust to me alone—that he was both amused and bemused by my bringing the negotiations to his country house doorstep.

I stood to greet him, and as I did, the two senior partners of the firm, Robert Smythe and Halston Senior, came in from a side door, in their hunting togs and carrying their rifles at the ready rest. I had really stepped into it here. This quite obviously was a gathering I was crashing. Still, the French negotiator had been invited. So, I would press on. The worst thing that could happen would be that my company would lose the bid—and it seemed to be doing that anyway if Sean Dupre was invited for the weekend and I wasn't.

I was desperate, and although I'd been skittish to try this ploy, desperate situations called for desperate means.

Neither of the senior partners seemed the least bit upset I was there and Hal Junior was still giving me his amused look.

"Must you bring your guns into the conservatory, Father Withers?" Hal's wife asked as her hand holding the tea pot was

poised over my cup. "You know I abhor firearms in the house."
Her delivery was calm and offhand, as if this was an old sore that
she knew wasn't going to be salved.

"Well, it's no longer my house, Muriel, and you seem to
have moved the gun cabinet. I couldn't find it. Perhaps you can
come show me where I can put my gun."

Mrs. Withers blushed, but, having finished pouring my
tea, she rose and said, "Shall we go up then?"

Robert Smythe broke in just as Muriel Withers and her
father-in-law were leaving the room with a blustered voice query
for Hal Junior. "Where's the Frenchie got off to? We were to go
for a ride after the hunt. I sure as hell hope he's better at that
than hunting."

"He's not bad, Bob. He's tied up upstairs; you can find
him in the Green Room, if you wish, though."

As Smythe headed for the main staircase hall, Eddie
leaned over to his sister, Vicki, and said, "I'm in the mood for
another game. Shall we?" And, with Vicki's consent, Hal Junior
and I were suddenly alone.

"Couldn't live without me, could you?" Hal said in a
quiet voice, that smile still on his face.

"Something like that. But we have some more
negotiating to do, I believe, before the fuller meeting with your
senior partners."

"Nothing would please me more," he said as he strode
over to me and leaned down. His mouth went to mine, and one
of his hands went to my basket.

"Business negotiation, Hal," I said, pulling away from
him—but not fast enough to fool him. He knew I was aching
for him in that sense. I opened the briefcase I'd brought in with
me, though, and took the photographs out.

"It occurred to me that these photographs work both
ways, Hal," I said. "I may not want my family and employers to
see these. But I assume you don't want your loved ones and
business associates to see them, either. I did my research and
know you have a family just as I do. It's fortuitous that your
senior partners are here this weekend too, though. This should
return us to completely equal grounds in the negotiations. So,
perhaps we can start all over again. My people have run all of the
95

numbers and we're confident we can give a much better deal than the French company can."

"You are trying to blackmail me with the photographs I took to blackmail you?" Hal asked. Then, before I could respond, he laughed out loud. "My god, that is cheeky, man. Cheeky and bold. I must say I like your style."

"Then shall we talk the deal again?" I asked, pleased that I had found the key to get the negotiations back on equal, at least, if not necessarily advantageous grounds.

"Come, stand up. I want to show you something," Hal said.

Warily, I stood. He took me by the hand and walked me out to the grand foyer and then up the side staircase that split half-way up. We took the right-hand split and then down a center hallway. The door to one of the rooms was slightly open, and Hal pushed it a bit more open. The overwhelming sensation I got when I looked into the room was the color green. A dark, rich green. The next sensation was the sound of full effort, wheezing sex. Only after that did my visual sense kick in to where I could see the young Frenchman, Sean Dupre, naked and on his back on the top of the bed, with his arms pulled above his head, his wrists tied to the top railing of the ornate headboard of the canopy bed and his legs stretched up and tied to the posters at the opposite corners of foot of the bed. Robert Smythe, equally naked, was standing between Dupre's thighs and fucking him with a great deal of huffing and puffing.

Now I knew what Hal had meant about Dupre being tied up and both Hal and Smythe had meant when they talked of going riding with the young Frenchman.

"As you can see," Hal said in sotto voce as he pulled the door to the Green Room to and pulled me out into the center of the hall, "Robert Smythe is still making up his mind about the bid. If he doesn't fall in love with Sean—and he is a very sweet young man, if not yet a seasoned negotiator—you may have an interview with Bob later this evening to try to win his vote. And, as you can see, our photographs aren't going to shock Bob one bit. Now, I believe the end of the hall is next. The Blue Room."

I almost gasped when we peeked into a larger bedroom suite at the end of the hallway, decorated in blue, when Hal quietly clicked the door open and I saw that his father was putting his personal gun away inside Hal's wife, Muriel, on another four-poster bed. She was bent over the bed on her belly and he was fucking her from behind doggy style. Her face showed almost a blank, this-is-my-duty neutral expression. His face was florid, but he obviously was enjoying himself.

"My father and I share and share alike, Doug," Hal said when we were back in the hallway. "So, you can see that my family is not likely to be intimidated by these photographs. And if you think that either my wife or my father will be shocked seeing me fuck another man, I must apprise you that I went to the best of English public schools—as did my father—and as did the men in my wife's family. We have quite a tradition of buggery in all of the best schools here, you know. My senior partners expect me to win the negotiations I take on for the firm—any way I can."

I was flabbergasted and couldn't quite manage to say anything.

"Now, I wonder if we'll find the young people in Vicki's or Eddie's rooms?"

"My god, you can't mean? . . . they went off to play tennis."

"Oh, neither one of them plays tennis," Hal said with a little laugh. "They just like to fuck in tennis gear. And don't looked so shocked. They aren't biologically related. Eddie is Muriel's from her first marriage and Vicki is mine from my first marriage. Now, come. Come to the other hallway. That's where my bedroom is. That's where you can give me your best bid—and I can enjoy fucking you again."

I gave him the best blow job I could muster as he lay back on the center of the red brocade-covered four-poster in the suite at the other end of the bedroom hall in what had to be the Red Room. And then I climbed over him and sank my channel on his cock and, my chest plastered to his, and raised my pelvis enough for Hal to do the fucking—because that's how he said he wanted to do it. Before he was finished, he turned me onto my back, pushed his knees under my rump to lift my channel to his cock and finished with deep, fast strokes.

"That was nice," he said when he was done. "You have much more experience than Sean does. I also like your initiative in not just leaving the negotiations to us. So, I'll tell you what. Show me the notes where your company registers the very lowest bid they've authorized you to make. We'll add five million to that, and if it's under the French company's open bid, you'll have my vote."

"Thank you," I moaned. "What I mean is thank you for the fuck. If you'll fuck me again, it sounds like it's a good deal."

"I'll be happy to do so tonight—if you still want me to after Bob Smythe and my father are finished with you. Both have said they want a crack at you. We can go on to the Green Room now, and I'll ride the Frenchie again while Smythe has his way with you. If I know my father, he won't be finished with Muriel until dinner time, but should be able to visit your room in the night. I think you'll be amazed at how well he fucks. I know I am. You will stay for dinner and the night, I hope."

I turned over and moaned—and then cried out—as Hal started to stuff what he could of fingers and fist in my channel. These would possibly be the hardest negotiations I'd ever conducted.

The Clothes Horse

"You'd get half of the bid, plus you'd get to keep the clothes."

I didn't know that I was all that wild about being auctioned off, but I had to admit that I liked—no, I loved—Zhao Zeng's clothes. That was what had attracted me to him in the first place. His black satin shirt and trousers were cut so well—and so provocatively—on him that I could hardly keep my eyes off him, even though I'd come into Hong Kong's Déjà Vu bar on Staunton Street on a members-only Friday night with a Dutch businessman who had picked me up in the lobby of the Butterfly on Wellington hotel and asked me to go up to his room with him.

He obviously had misjudged that I was a male hooker when I'd only ducked into that hotel lobby to get out of a brief rain shower, but I was horny, liked older men, and he was good looking, so I went with him.

It wasn't the money part of Zhao Zeng's auction deal, when he got around to pitching the deal to me, that turned me off. I had found the misconception that I was a rent boy arousing. The Dutch guy, who I was happy to find was pretty limber, had given me 500 Hong Kong dollars—the equivalent of about $60 U.S.—to go up to his room and bang him hard. Which I did. He made so much of a to do about my musculature that I took him with me standing in the middle of the hotel room and supporting his weight wrapped around my pelvis, his legs hooked above my rump, and pulled him on and off my cock while he whimpered and gasped. Before I was finished, I made him lower his torso toward the carpet and grab my ankles, and I jack hammered down into him, with him crying that I was too big for him to take but that, no, he didn't want me to stop. At least that's what I took what he was blubbering in Dutch to mean.

I almost laughed when he offered me another 1,000 Hong Kong dollars to stay the night.

I'll bet he couldn't stand up straight the next day, although he seemed to manage well enough for a second round before we left the hotel room. I put him into a party mood, and he wanted to show me off, he said. So we were doing the rounds of the gay bars, where we would sit for a drink or two with his cronies and he'd let them cop a feel of me so they could appreciate how lucky he was that night. He also, I think, was trying to impress me with his private club membership privileges on the island. He said he wanted me to stay with him for a while and maybe to take a cruise to Macao on his yacht.

I told him no thanks and, no, it wasn't because he was twice my age.

He asked me if it was because of the young, well-dressed Chinese man I'd been sharing looks with at the Déjà Vu, and I'd said that, of course it wasn't. But I was lying about that.

So, when Zhao came up with his proposal, it wasn't the fucking older men part that had me hesitating—I'd just done a middle-aged, albeit in shape, Dutch businessman for 500 HK. What had me going was being sold like a piece of meat without me picking out who I wanted to fuck. Zhao Zeng had told me I could turn the trick down, though, if I didn't like who had given the highest bid for me.

But then I wouldn't get the clothes. And it was the clothes that I was interested in having. I could buy clothes back in Bangkok, where I was a Marine guard in the U.S. Embassy—

and well-cut clothes too. But I hadn't seen anything there that could show off my physique as good as what Zhao Zeng wore into the Déjà Vu bar showed off his.

It was only when Zhao took me to his apartment above his shop later that night that I found out that he himself had designed and cut the clothes he was wearing.

I was on R&R from Bangkok. There was plenty of guy-on-guy action to be had there, of course, and I had become a favorite in the gay expatriate crowd and the upper classes of the Thai because of how I was built, keeping well toned up because I was a twenty-year-old Marine and that was part of being a Marine, and because of what I was packing—and how I was able to use it. But I was always looking over my shoulder in Thailand, wondering when I'd be outed and sent home. Going home wasn't a big problem with me—even leaving the Marines wasn't. My dad owned a garage, and I liked tinkering with cars—and also tinkering with men who owned sports cars and who were willing to pay for their fucks. But I'd found a good thing in Asia with the free-and-loose societies here, and I didn't want to have to go home before I'd had a lot of fun.

I'd heard I could have a lot of fun if I took my R&R in Hong Kong. And I'd only been here the better part of a day and already had topped a hotel bell boy—who had a hole I almost needed mining equipment to get into, although, once in, he knew how to maximize my pleasure—and a Dutch businessman, the latter profitably, so I could see that Hong Kong was going to be a lot of fun.

I liked fucking Asians. It was particularly nice in Bangkok, where a lot of the men were such little guys that it would seem that my thick eight and a half inches would devastate them, but who always proved they could take me and make it interesting—just like the Butterfly hotel bell hop had done—and would continue to do every night I returned to the hotel.

Zhao was compact like a lot of the Thai guys were. He was a good foot shorter than I was, but that didn't make him a midget. I was a full six foot five. And, although he was perfectly proportioned, he was slim and what I'd call willowy. Again, this was a lot like many of the Thai guys. I was to find too that he was more experienced in sex than the Thai men I had fucked. My size intimidated most of them, and they tended to become like rag dolls underneath me when I fucked them. Zhao took control and played every aspect of me in the sex act. He wasn't afraid of my muscled body and big dick—he worshipped them and showed that he fully appreciated how I had developed my body

The Dutch businessman was meaty in comparison, although I wouldn't have called him fat. And he was a lot older. He was good looking, though, and had been the boldest of the guys in the lobby of the Butterfly in approaching me, so it had been fine going with him. And he proved to be flexible enough to make the fuck fun.

In comparison with Zhao for what I liked, though, he was second or third best.

He also was philosophical about my changing horses at the bar. He'd had a standing fuck like he said he'd never gotten before, and I'd been very good to him for his 500 HK.

My eyes went to Zhao as soon as he entered the bar. He looked both sexy and elegant in his black satin outfit, which fit him like a glove. He came to the bar and, after ordering a drink, turned and surveyed the room. The Dutch businessman and I were at a table with some of the Dutchmen's business cronies, and Zhao's eyes lingered when they moved to me. They slitted, and I could tell that he was seeing the two of us together. So, I got up from my table and slid up to the bar, where we could contemplate being together closer.

I could hear him gasp from across the room when I stood and he'd been able to see the extra thickness running down my left thigh from my groin inside my tight jeans. I didn't know at the time that this had such an effect on him—but at the time I didn't know how expert he was in how clothes fit a man.

"American?" he asked when I'd bellied up to the bar to refresh my drink and that of the Dutchman, as well, who now was lost in trading business stories with the other businessmen at our table.

"Yes," I answered. "Visiting from Bangkok, where I work at the American embassy."

"You are in superb shape. Do you do modeling?"

"I haven't. I must ask whether you are a model yourself, though—and where did you get those great clothes?"

"No, I'm not a model. Would you like to see more clothes like this—maybe some you can try on yourself—at my flat nearby?"

"You don't engage in much foreplay, do you?"

"Not when I see what I want."

"Unfortunately, I'm with someone," I said, as the barman delivered the drinks to me I'd come up to the bar to fetch.

"Pity," Zhao man said as I pushed off from the bar.

About twenty minutes later when I went to the men's room while the Dutchman and his friends were trading boasts in French, which I didn't speak, and thus was not interested in the conversation, I no sooner had unzipped and pulled my cock out than the young Chinese man came in and stood near me at the urinal.

"No, don't turn away," he whispered to me. "Let me watch you, please."

I found him attractive, so I half turned to him and let him watch me piss into the urinal, and when I was finished, he reached over and took my cock in his hand. I started to go hard immediately. He had his thumb on my piss slit and was gently rubbing that and jacking my cock with slender fingers running down the underside of my shaft. He moved his other hand up the front of my shirt, deftly opening buttons as he did so and then running his hand over the contours of my torso muscles, giving the impression that he was making a mold of my musculature. All the time he was murmuring how magnificently cut my body was.

"They have rooms in the back," he said. "Will you come with me?"

"What, now?"

"Yes, please. You have a magnificent body and a strong, manly face. I would like to clothe you and have you model for me."

"You want me to go with you to a room in the back so you can clothe me and I can model for you?"

"Later, yes, if you're interested. But now I would like you to cover me."

"Cover you? You mean fuck you?"

"Yes, please. You have a beautiful body. I would make it worth your while. I would make a suit for you—one that would fit you like a glove. I would be proud to have my label on such a perfect body."

Throughout this exchange he had been slowly pumping my cock, and I was breathing a bit hard and was otherwise very hard. I was sorely tempted, but I didn't walk out on a guy just because a more tempting one walked by.

"Sorry, but I came here with someone. Tonight wouldn't work out for me."

"But you would come with me if you were free? You cover men, don't you?"

"Yes, I would come. And yes I top men."

"You would . . . top . . . . me?"

"Yes. I find you very arousing. I just can't tonight."

"I think you are about ready to ejaculate. May I take that now and then we can discuss something more?"

Without asking, he was sinking his knees to the floor, taking my cock in his mouth, and for the three minutes it took me to come down his throat, I was lost to his expert attentions.

When I returned to my Dutchman, I'm not sure he realized I had ever been gone. I told him I had to go someplace for a while and that I would come back to his room at the hotel later, and he was so oft hand about agreeing to that that I'm not sure he even remembered we had made the assignation. He was steeped in drink and bantering conversation with his business friends. I had been displayed already; he'd gotten whatever good impression he wanted from having me with him.

I rose from the table and went back to where Zhao was sitting at the bar. "How far away is this apartment of yours?"

It wasn't far away at all—just about three blocks. We entered through a shop front. The shop itself was handsomely appointed. The clothes on the male mannequins rising up from the racks and low shelves of men's folded clothes were even handsome. And so sexy.

The second story displayed even more intimate apparel. I walked around fingering this and that. I particularly liked the mesh wear.

"Do you own this shop?" I asked.

"Yes. And I design the clothes. Do you like them?"

"Yes, I do. The ones on this floor give me a hard-on, if you must know."

"I am happy to hear that. And I would be pleased to do something about that. But first, would you mind if I clothed you and took some photographs? If you allow me to do that, you can have what I pick out for you to wear."

I hesitated a moment and Zhao picked up a black mesh body suit that left little to the imagination. I then said I would be happy to be photographed in exchange for the clothes. And, although I apologized, Zhao was happy that I had a raging hard-on for the photographs.

The photo shoot was on the fifth floor of his shop, which evidently was the first floor of an apartment that went up more floors. The third floor had been his cutting room and the fourth a storage room. The fifth was mostly one large room too, with a kitchen unit on one wall. A velvet-covered platform with camera lights and video machines on tripods surrounding it was in the center of the room and from this a raised runway led off to the back of the floor and a doorway through the only wall partitioning off an area from the larger room. The rest of the room was outfitted with deep, wide sofas and armless upholstered chairs with sloping backs that looked like provocative support for inventive fuck positions—which, as it turned out, was exactly what they were for. The floor was covered with deep-pile carpeting in a light beige, and large, silk pillows were thrown around, apparently haphazardly, but, I was sure, with studied precision.

This was obviously a party room—and a show room for patrons to view clothing being modeled.

Zhao photographed me sprawled on the platform and masturbating myself, with my cock poking out of a slit in the mesh bodysuit. And then, when I was hard for him, he set the video cameras in motion, and I fucked him on the platform.

He moaned deeply when he got the full view of what I was packing, and he groaned and grunted when he felt the full measure of what I could do with it.

I took him three ways—missionary style, doggy fuck, and side split—before I was worked up enough to ejaculate, all while the cameras were rolling.

Zhao marveled during the first fuck position, as I stroked him shallow—although he moaned like I was taking him deep—and he fisted the root of my cock that I wasn't burying and rotated my cock to give him maximum rub on his prostate with my bulb. He cried for mercy when I fucked him deep and fast in the doggy position. But I gave him no quarter—and he loved it. The side split was languid and included kissing and mutual gliding and prodding of hands on each other's bodies until we came together.

Zhao was as expert in taking the cock as I was in giving it. He declared he'd never been taken by anyone as young and powerful and cut as I was, and I complimented him on his ability to sheath more than eight inches and to work a cock with his channel muscles.

It was after that, when he told me how much he had enjoyed me, that he set the unusual proposition.

"How long will you be in Hong Kong?"

"A week, maybe eight days."

"Are you interested in model sex in exchange for clothes and half the bid your services bring?"

"I don't understand."

"Do you want your pick of the clothes I make?"

"You know I want your clothes. You've seen how well I like them—what I was willing to do to get this mesh bodysuit."

"My clothes are exclusive and they are very expensive. But if you model for my private showings for interested men, and fuck the man who bids the highest for your services at the end of the runway show, you can keep half of the money that's bid and the clothes you wore on the runway. I think I can arrange three viewing parties while you are in Hong Kong."

"I don't see myself as a runway model," I answered, with a laugh. "I'm a bit more beefy than the male models I've seen."

"You will be the hit of the show. I have a few regular models who will also be there. But I predict you will receive the highest bids."

He was right. I received the highest bids, fucked six well-heeled middle-aged men on Zhao's king-sized bed on the sixth floor or on those curvy armchairs on the showroom level, while he—and sometimes another male model—was also being fucked on the bed. And I came away with eight great outfits, including a two-outfit bonus because, Zhao said, I had performed so well and turned an amazingly large profit for him.

It wasn't just dumpy older men who Zhao invited to his runway parties either. He was as discerning in the men he invited to watch, bid, and play as he was in the precise cutting of his clothes. I would have happily gone with any of these men in Bangkok just for the fuck. I liked older, wealthy and self-confident men, and I liked fucking older men who melted at being taken by a fit, young Marine. It was all gravy on this gig and all of them were rich enough to offer astonishing sums for my cocking—and I got to keep the clothes I had modeled for them.

Whenever I came out in an outfit, Zhao would call me his "clothes horse." I asked him about this later, and he laughed and said, "That's a signal at my parties. Although the patrons could see it themselves in the cut of the clothes you wore, the significant word there was 'horse.' I use this term to denote a certain level of endowment, and the men set their bidding up appropriately to be able to enjoy the extra length and girth. This, plus your magnificent physique, set the bidding at levels I've never received before."

I returned to Bangkok with three times the money I'd gone on R&R with and a great, sexy wardrobe, along with having my desire for an exotic, free-spirited exercise of my cock, and with an agreement to come back for my R&R next year. Zhao said he loved the Marine in me, and I said I knew of a couple more of the Marine guards at the Bangkok embassy who might like the same deal.

The Dutch businessman was, fortuitously, on the same flight back to Bangkok that I was on. I modeled my new wardrobe for him in his room at the Dusit Thani, gave him another hard, inventive-position 5,000 Thai baht fuck, and barely made it back to Marine House before the last minute of my memorable R&R was up.

Yep, I love my Asian tour—and my nifty new wardrobe.

The Video List

"It sounds too complicated for you, Matt," Jason had said. "Getting a list would be the hardest part—impossible, I think. This is a small potatoes town. I think you should just keep it to the street and be happy when it works out. And get a job."

I'll admit that getting a job was what got the plan rolling. Then getting a list turned out to be one of the easiest parts. The roughest part, speaking of rough, was Mr. Gordon that first time and then through all the takes needed to get the video recorded just the way he wanted it.

I first started thinking that something needed to change in my life when two guys in a row took the blow job in their cars and then just pushed me out on the ground, outside town, rather than paying—and left me to hitchhike back. Griff, the guy who got me started thinking about changing my approach, saying I was a natural in looks to turn guys on who were looking for it, did tell me that I should at least move to Richmond, or better, down to Atlanta to do the street work. But I didn't have the money to go that far in any direction yet. That's why I was working the street; I needed the money.

He told me that there was a system for this in the big cities, sort of a recognized behavior for a john to take on—unless you ran into some crazy guy who wanted to do it and then cut you up. But you could usually tell that by their eyes and the sort of smile they had on their face, Griff said. And if they were driving some beat-up old heap. Look for the guys with the new Mustangs and Bimmers, he said. The guys in the Mustangs would give you a good fuck, and the guys in the Bimmers would give you a good tip. Small-town johns didn't seem to know the rules, Griff said. A lot of them were too dumb to realize they'd want it more than once and that there weren't a whole lot of young guys walking the streets who would give it to them once they got a reputation as welchers—or as being too rough and abusive.

That didn't stop those two men in a row from getting their blow jobs and then pushing me out of the car. And I didn't have time for that. Neither one was Mr. America, either. Griff had told me I shouldn't get in the business if I didn't like to get cocked. I told him I liked it fine. I didn't tell him, though, that I wasn't real wild about kissing any frogs in the process—least wise not unless they were good tippers.

There were a whole lot of frogs down here in south central Virginia. At least most of them were built. It was hard making a living down here—which goes back to my original problem—and most jobs in these parts required a whole lot of muscle. I could like being cocked by a guy with muscle even if he had a frog face. Where I usually gave it was in a truck bed out in a forest road at night. There usually was only one muscle I got to see up close and if it was big and fat, that's usually all I needed.

I did, though, prefer doing it inside with a guy who was a looker as well as built. And I kinda liked guys in their forties, if they'd taken good care of themselves. They tended to take it slower and to make sure they took care of me better. They also usually showed that they were grateful that someone would still give it to them.

This all led up to Mr. Gordon and then the idea of the lists. But before that was the opportunity to get off the streets and into a job, which, in the end, made everything else possible.

I got a job working in a video store—an adult video store. And this was one that catered to all interests. The gay section was in a back room. That got pretty good foot traffic, because it was the only adult video store in three counties that also had a gay section.

I got the job because the owner of the store, a middle-aged fat black man who lived over in Lynchburg and had a string of shops like this fanned out across southside Virginia, pulled me off street duty one night and fucked me in the backseat of his old pimpmobile Cadillac. While he was sitting in the middle of the backseat and I was facing him, riding his cock, he was telling me what a nice little piece I was. And then he got the idea that maybe I'd like to work in his video store in the next town—that he'd then know where I was if and when he got a hankering to have me again.

Yes, of course I would like that. I was looking for a job that would mean I didn't have to work the streets and hope for a couple of twenties humping the dicks of frogs like him in the backseats of their cars.

I'd already told Jason that I had plans to be making more money with my body than I was making now. I couldn't tell Griff the sort of ideas I was having, because he'd already left for Charlotte. In the end the video list idea turned out better than anything else I was thinking.

The job at the video store was OK. I had the afternoon-to-early-evening shift. That gave me time afterward to turn a trick or two out on the street most nights. That already was better than only working the streets. Sometimes after roaming around the back gay section for a while and working their need up, some of the guys would ask me if I'd blow them or let them blow me for money. This was better than the street, because we did it in the stockroom rather than out in the back of someone's car—and because I'd make them let me lock their wallets up in the drawer under the cash register first so that we both knew they weren't going to get it and then walk out without paying. But the money was still penny-ante. Usually not more than fifteen dollars—and that only for the big spenders—for a blow job, one way or the other. I didn't think it was safe enough to leave the shop long enough for an ass fuck, even though I was asked for that too. I rarely got above twenty dollars for that when I did do it.

That was pretty insulting. They were standing with both me and them in full light. In the light of the video shop they could see exactly what they were getting. I knew I was desirable to a man. But most of them were frogs and still didn't want to pay much. Those who were hunks wanted it for free. Of course, some of them got it for free, after my shift was over, in the backseats of their cars at the back edge of the parking lot. I wouldn't have been doing this at all if I didn't like being cocked regularly.

But Mr. Gordon. He broke the ice on that—and from there was born the video list idea.

He showed up a couple of times to browse the aisles in the back room. He even bought a few videos. Mr. Gordon was what I would call a Mr. America hunk—but of twenty years ago. He was probably in his forties, but he was built like he worked out half the day. His head was bald—which I have a theory about, that it gives a man extra umpf "down there," which so far has proved to be true—and he looked a little mean. I think it was the hard angles of his face—he was a bit of frog there—but also the tattooing that peeked out below his shirt sleeves and inside the V neck of the polo shirts he liked to wear—pulled real tight across his chest, showing the nubs of his nipples, the outline of thick nipple rings, and how well his torso came down to a flat belly. He liked to chat me up when he was in the shop, and after a few visits, I got the impression he came more to chat me up than to buy videos. In fact, he got real picky about buying those.

"I can make better videos than that myself, in my own studio."

"You've got your own film studio?" I asked

"Yeah. Right where I live. You know that old motel out on the Richmond road?"

"The one with the gym that's been built on the end of it?"

"Yeah, that one. I built the gym and I've made a house for myself by stringing four of the motel rooms together. There are a couple of empties, but I went ahead and had them made into bedroom units too. On the other end of the string of rooms, I've got a photo studio set up—a darkroom and a studio. All outfitted and everything. I'm always looking for models. I've filmed some guys from the gym. They'd make better porn stars than a lot of guys on these tapes."

"Porn stars? That's . . . uh . . . interesting."

"Bet a video of one of those guys working you real good could be a best-seller."

I didn't know what to say. He caught me by surprise on that one. He didn't give me much time to come up with anything to say, either.

"I seen you on the street. That's right, ain't it? I seen you working the street."

"Yeah, so?" Even though I responded this time, I still hadn't come up with anything brilliant to say.

"Pretty little guy like you, all innocent face and everything, and young lookin'. I bet a video of a muscle guy working you over would sell real well. How much they pay you on the street for it? Fifty dollars or so?"

"No, they don't pay me any fifty dollars," I said, trying to sound indignant—trying not to sound pathetic because no one had paid me anything close to that for anything.

"I seen you lookin' at me when I come through here. You're interested in my tats, ain't you? And I seen you lookin' close at my chest. Can see the tit rings, can't you? Wonder where else I got them, don't you?"

I was hanging on to the edge of the counter across from him, trying not to hyperventilate. But I bet he could tell by the way I was trembling and how white my knuckles were in gripping the edge of the counter that he had my attention.

He pulled his polo shirt over his head.

"Oh . . . holy . . . shit," I murmured. The guy had an old naval battle being reenacted all over his torso and down his arms. Wooden ships with sails and everything and cannon fire bursts.

"Like the nipple rings?" he asked. "Got a thicker ring in the cock. Bet you wonder how big the cock is. Let's you and me make a movie and you can find out how big it gets."

* * * *

He had video cameras on tripods pointed at all four sides of the blue-velvet-covered platform in the middle of his studio room—and one pointed down from the ceiling—while he rough fucked the stuffing out of me in four long takes. It took much of the night. He wore a black mask, but other than that all that he wore was the tattoo undulating in a sea battle lasting a couple of hours—and his body jewelry. I wore nothing but animated facial expressions of being taken repeatedly and deeply by a big, thick, pistoning cock with a thick ring in it that I had wondered if I'd be able to feel working inside me—and I did.

He said the facial expressions would sell the video all by themselves. And when he'd gotten everything spliced together and edited I could see what he meant. I came in my jeans just watching myself getting fucked like that on tape.

The sequence of me sitting on the side of the platform and sucking his cock while he stood there, hands back on his hips so the cameras got the best shot, was, he said, to show how big the cock was that was going to be working inside me. After that, it was all business: three three-minute teasers starting with me on my belly, facing a camera, and showing in my face what I thought of him looming in the camera frame behind me, his big hands gripping my waist, and fucking my ass hard and deep. This was the shot angle he put into the video, saying my expressions were worth a million. The next sequence was taken from behind his muscled, tapering back and bulbous butt cheeks, with him between my thighs while I was on my back on the platform, and him holding my legs spread up and wide with fists gripping my ankles. There was a break away in this to the opposite side, showing my head flopped over to the side, with an expression of "I'm in heaven, but it's a heaven of an eight-inch, ringed cock up my ass" on my face. The fade out here is me shooting cum in the air.

The third segment was him on the platform on his back and my back to his chest. He had his arms laced under my pits, imprisoning my arms over my head and his legs were forcing mine out. He made sure that the base of his cock could be seen by the camera as it appeared and disappeared while he was

114

fucking up into me. Once again he said that my expressions were what sold the film. To get those, while he was fucking me, he was telling me about what he was going to do with me later that night in his bedroom, where he had frames on his bed and a sling and velvet cuffs.

The video ended with me on my back and his straddling my chest. He was stroking himself, ready to come and had fisted the hair on my head and brought my head up close to his cock so that he could come on my face. The fadeout was of me taking the cock in my mouth and cleaning it.

He was good as his word. After cleaning up his studio, he took me into the house he'd made in the center of the motel and to a bedroom that had everything he said it did. There were cameras here too, but he didn't turn them on. He said he needed to find out where my edges were before we could talk about making that type of film. Through the night he used all of the equipment, including a lash and what he called ball busters, and the bindings—and I found out what he meant about where the edges were.

I'd never been fucked like that before—like what happened during the filming in the studio and certainly not like what happened later in his bedroom.

I was—and am—ready to do it again.

He paid me two-hundred dollars for the night—for the film and then anything he wanted to do with me for the rest of the night. It was more money than I'd ever made in a night. In all, four three-minute scenes faded together, with a two-minute explosive ending. Fifteen minutes.

"I can make more films—longer ones—from the material I have here," he said at breakfast in his kitchen. "This can be something like a teaser. I'll pay you a percentage on the films."

"A teaser, you say?" Suddenly everything fell into place for me, like the tumblers on those wall safes that spies have to get into within seconds on TV programs. "I might have a better, bigger idea."

"I like to hear better, bigger ideas," he answered.

"You say you have a few unused motel rooms."

"Yeah, three."

When I unrolled my whole plan to him, he was enthusiastic, and we celebrated a new partnership by him carrying me back to his bed, slamming me down on my back, jerking my legs open, scooting his knees under my buttocks to raise my pelvis to the perfect angle to take the full-in slide of his cock, and my tracing the undulating ships on the waves on his chest, set in movement by the pistoning of his cock deep inside me.

Jason was a harder sell on the idea.

"I don't get it. It all revolves around having a list. A customer's list. I told you that would be nearly impossible to build."

"Look at this, Jason," I said. We were standing at the counter in the video store and I showed him a chart on a clipboard.

"Yeah, OK. E-mail addresses on a list," he said in derision. "That's nothing concrete."

"These are guys who come into the back room who I like the looks of. Luckily I like the looks of rich-looking older guys. I smile at them and wink and tell them if they are interested in receiving a special treat, to put an e-mail address down, and I'll send it to them. Most I offer that to put the e-mail address down. It doesn't matter if it's not the e-mail address they use in their straight life. If the e-mail reaches them, that's all that's needed."

"Yeah, so. Then you send them a copy of that video you made and they get their rocks off. What's in it for you?"

"The e-mail back to them tells them they can play too for a hundred dollars for a fuck and twenty-five dollars an hour for a room to do it in."

"And you think anybody's going to bite on that? You've been fucking guys on the street for thirty dollars a hump. I've been doing it for twenty-five. What makes you think anyone will pay a hundred for it, plus room charge?"

"Have you been hearing the dinging in the background while we've talked about this, Jason? We sent out copies of the videos—Mr. Gordon got a list going at his gym too—so that they'd arrive yesterday or today. There were five e-mail responses on the computer when I came in this afternoon. Since then the incoming has been hopping up and down."

"Yeah, OK, but there's only so much that you can—"

"The rooms, Jason. There are three rooms available in Mr. Gordon's layout. He's having doors cut into them from the rear parking lot. I've already called Griff. He's on his way back from Charlotte."

"Oh, uh . . ."

"The third room, Jason. That's why I'm talking to you. That third room could be for you. Of course there'd have to be a teaser video made with Mr. Gordon first. Did I tell you he has a thick cock ring—and an even thicker cock—and that you can watch a sea battle while he fucks you?"

The Celtic Sonata of Life

I was sitting outside the cottage door, just in my shorts, wondering if the farmer who had rented the rustic Cotswold cottage with the thatched roof and the rose trellis beside the door to me for two weeks had misinterpreted my offer. It hadn't been in so many words, but I think I had been clear enough in my nonverbal delivery. But maybe not. Maybe signaling here in England was much different from how it was in the States.

I had been antsy with my writing, not being able to make much progress. Back in New York, I would have known what I needed to break the blockage: attention from one of the muscle men in the gym down on the first floor of my building. I would go downstairs and stand in the doorway. They would see and understand what I needed, and one of the hunks would put his bar bells down, climb the stairs with me, and fuck the stuffing out of me. Then I would give him the proverbial pat on the head and send him back to the gym. After that I could and would write all night. I never had a problem finding someone down there who wanted me. I always was in control.

The Gloucestershire farmer had reminded me of the men in the gym, but more honestly built, less malleable perhaps, and a man of determination. A bit of danger for someone like me, who wanted to call all of the shots. He was a man of the fields, big and bulky, but built like a bodybuilder. His muscles were, I'm sure, the result of hard work on the land rather than the artifice of the gym. His cottage had been listed on a gay-friendly Web site, and it had rather explicitly indicated that single, young, gay men were preferred. So I had hope that there would be something to be had from him while I hid away in the Cotswolds and tried to make progress on my book. A bit of dalliance when it pleased me. When I saw him, standing by the cottage door this morning, when I drove up, I almost melted. He was big and beautiful in a brutish, stubbornly arrogant way. I had occasion to hope there would be something from him for me, and even more reason to hope that when he told me that he was single, that he lived alone, and that he worked the farm himself.

I told him I was gay and a writer, and that I had come to write, not to sightsee. I asked him if he was a reader, but he said he was more of a music listener—and a dancer. I had visions of him clogging away at a village fair and regretted that he wasn't a reader. If he had read my books, he would have known what I wanted from a man like him, what I expected from a man who wanted to go with me. I told him, still hopeful, that I worked mainly at night at the computer and that my mornings, such as they were, were spent spinning the stories in my mind. But the evenings, I said, I usually liked to be away from the writing. I often read in the evening, or talked with someone, if someone was there to talk to.

"I dance in the evenings," he said, simply. From the first moment, he was direct, straightforward, with me, not the least anxious to fit in with my plans.

I thought then that he hadn't taken the hint—or, worse, had caught the invitation and had rejected it. I was a bit miffed. I wasn't used to being rejected. But then, this was England, not the United States. I recognized that tastes could be different by differing location. He looked like he probably fancied someone rougher, less complex, less sophisticated than I was. I had visions that while I was reading in the evening, he would be in the village dancing, probably clogging. I don't know why I thought they clogged in this region, but it seemed to go with the atmospherics here. Everything was rural. Beautiful, but rural. The farmer seemed rural too. Very basic, probably his whole life devoted to his farm. Rural but beautiful. But seeing him in my mind dancing some silly village dance lessened his appeal to me. Otherwise I probably wouldn't have given up earlier in the day before he set off for his fields; I'd have been at his door asking for a cup of whiskey or something—with the emphasis on the "something."

The twilight was so inviting that I was sitting at the cottage door next to the rose trellis, using the light streaming through the doorway of the essentially one-room cottage to light my page. I had only read a few pages when I saw him approaching.

He was all cleaned up, a bottle of some liquor—probably a local brew—in his hand. He was stripped to the waist, wearing baggy farmer's trousers below, which only accentuated the hard, barrel chest and tapering down the torso to flat abs telling the tale of what a serious six pack meant. I gasped at the sight of him, not only the massive musculature of his torso, magnificently cut, but because he had tattooing of roses running down his chest—roses that matched the color of those on the rose trellis next to where I sat.

"I thought you danced in the evenings," I said in a low, wanting voice as he approached me.

"I do. I think you should dance tonight rather than read. I have come to dance."

He had also brought CDs. They surprised me. No clogging music here—whatever that was. Not even any fast music. All slow, sensuous, strangely unfamiliar music to me. Sounds of haunting instruments I could not identify and what were either other instrumental sounds or voices in the background, I could not tell which, as well blended in the rest of the music as it was. Behind it all, a good beat. Not a beat that I heard from the beginning, but a beat that became stronger as the evening unraveled.

"The music. Very strange," I said. "Almost primeval."

"It's Celtic music. It's what I dance to. It is music we use to make love to, out here on the farms."

Visions of fertility dances in the fields zipped through my brain. How could I use this image in my novels?

We were inside at that point, him standing by the CD player and me sitting on the edge of the bed. There were straight chairs in the room, and a small table near the kitchen bar, but not room for much else. Just a square of space in the center of the room. While standing at the CD player, he undid his belt buckle, unbuttoned his fly, and let his farmer's wide-legged trousers sink to the floor.

Just like that. Straightforward, direct. Sure of himself. Knowing that what he had gave him entry where he wanted to go. Arrogance unbounded.

I moaned. He was in half erection, already magnificent. His thighs were beefy, but all muscle, strong as oaks. The vining from the rose trellis tattoo continued down across his smooth-shaved groin, and wrapped around the base of his cock. He had taken a handful of small packets and a tube of something out of the pocket of his trousers before they fell to the floor, and as I watched, he placed the tube and some of the packets on the table, opened the packet he still was holding, and rolled the condom on his cock. There was no question what he wanted— or that he had plans to get it more than once, if he fancied doing so. For the first time I felt that decisions, control were not mine here. We clearly were on his turf.

No courting here. This was the farm. Do your business and get back to work. I was the business that he would do this evening. Lonely on the farm? Invite a young man to use your cottage and get your rocks off covering him, again and again, if you wanted to. Leave him moaning on his back, unable to close his legs, and go back to the fields whistling.

I shuddered, conflicted by both desire and fear.

He walked to the center of the room. "Come, dance with me." He was holding an arm out, in invitation.

"I don't dance. Well, not well," I answered, my voice more of a croak than as I would have him hear it.

"You can dance with me. I will lead. I will control."

I bet you will was my thought. I was trembling. I barely could make it up to my feet. I took one step.

"No, take the shorts off first. I want to see you." and when I had fumbled my way out of the shorts, "Ah, you are a right sexy piece, you are. Turn around. Nice arse that. Plump. Should hole straight and true, and something to grab onto during the slide. I am glad you have booked for two weeks. And you are showing me that you want to dance with me. We will be good dance partners together."

Just a sexy piece with a nice, plump "arse" to slide into. Just verbal running of the farmer's hands down the flanks of the livestock. Good breeding stock. The dance crap just so much subterfuge. Not that that mattered, he was such a prime example of manhood. But that cock . . . the size of that.

"I admit I want to . . . but I am frightened. You are so large . . . I'm not accustomed . . ."

"You will love the dance. Come. You answered the advert. We both know what you wanted when you came here. We will both be happy, I'm sure. This is why I make the effort to have this cottage to rent. I make it sound like I prefer single-tenant gay men. If I like the look of them, I cock them. They never complain that I have."

"That's rather forward. I—"

"You want me to put you on the cock, don't you? You nearly ate me up showing that want earlier today."

I shimmered with uncontrollable arousal at the image of that—made more graphically fascinating by the size of him. It was the writer in me. Too much imagination."Yes," I answered in a small voice. I couldn't lie. And I was already naked before him, my need and want obvious.

"We dance the Dance of the Fuck, then. Now."

I shuddered when he took me into his arms. He was taller, bulkier, more powerfully built than I was. I had to stand on my tiptoes as, in a close embrace, we moved, back and forth, and against each other. His cock pressed into the center of my chest, into the base of my rib cage. He was gripping my wrists and moved my arms behind me, holding them together at the base of the small of my back. I felt the index finger of one of his hands move down into the upper crack of my buttocks.

The finger was not reaching the rim of my hole, but I found myself wanting it to, rising as much as I could to give it access. It was rubbing inside my cleft, though, and I was opening just at the sensation of him being so close to the quick of me.

I knew I was going to be fucked. I wanted it. He was making me ache for it. All self-assurance, no doubt he knew that. He had made clear he had caught my signaling from that morning. We both knew what he was here to do, what I was here to give him, to take from him.

His lips went to the hollow of my throat. We had moved close to the table where the CD player was resting in the undulation of our bodies in the slow, sensuous dance. I realized only now that this table had been a goal of his. He released my hands, and I sensed him handling something on the table top. As we moved away from the table again, toward the center of the room, I realized what it was he was doing. His hands were wet and slick now.

We stood, in the center of the room, just rocking back and forth with, against each other. His cock was rock hard against my rib cage. I knew mine was too. It was throbbing.

"Yes, yes, yesss," I murmured as I felt his large hands spanning my buttocks cheeks, squeezing and separating them.

"Oh, god, yesss," I whimpered, as I felt a finger from each hand, wet and slippery, circling my rim. And then slowly entering me, and pressing on my rim, opening me up.

"Loose. Used. But not loose enough yet for the likes of me."

Do you have to say every thought out loud? I screamed in my mind. Must you be so casual and coldblooded about it? But then I realized that his language, his actions, the matter-of-fact way he was going about it was much of what was making me melt to him, what was putting me under his power.

Standing and rocking against each other. Aware more now of the music. We were moving to the beat of the music. Or rather, the beautiful farmer was moving us to the rhythm of the music. Controlling, just as he had said he would. And the beat. Becoming more aware that there was a beat at the base of the music, coming more to the foreground.

More fingers, deeper, Spreading me open. I had never felt so open, so slack. I buried my face in his shoulder and panted hard. Roses. My eyes were fixated on the roses, curving with the curve of his hard pecs. A nipple in the center of one rose. This. I would write about this.

"A nice arse. A good hole for it. Tight enough to give me a good feel of it, but open enough for the deep slide and the working of it."

To me, the beating of my heart, more aware to me now too, was matching the beat of the music.

I couldn't help it. I couldn't wait. I ejaculated between his thighs. I was mortified, and buried my face harder into his shoulder, voicing a shuddered, "Sorry."

He gave a low laugh. "No worry. I will make you come again . . . and again. A good hole for it, for a good poke, time and again."

I moaned in anticipation. His lips found mine, and a third finger on each hand invaded my ass, pressing at the rim, coaxing me more open. Pushing my butt cheeks apart with the broad, calloused palms of his hands.

His lips disengaged from mine and went to my ear. "I am putting you to the cock now. You are open enough, I think. If not, I have something that will stretch you to fit soon enough. Maybe not the first time, but afterwards. The dick is wanting its hole something fierce."

"Yes, oh, god, yes," I moaned. Such bald language, arousing now that I was being worked—like the matter-of-fact way he had declared he was going to fuck me. Probably straightforward because of the nearness of a farmer to the basic functions and realities of life. Also because he was fully aware of who he was, what he had, what men like me wanted from him, whether we ourselves fully understood that or not. Intoxicating. Enough so that I didn't consider the ominous "I have something that will stretch you."

"Raise your right leg to my hip," he whispered. "You'll ride the cock with me standing the first time, I think. You'll enjoy it; it gives a good angle. Not a full slide, but we can get to that in time. A right good ass; I'll want to use it more."

Shaking almost uncontrollably, I raised my calf to his hip. Still clutching, spreading, my buttocks with his hands, fingers still inside my entrance, rubbing and coaxing the rim to expand, he lifted me and crouched a bit, with a thigh pressing into me under the leg I had lifted.

I felt the bulb of his cock at my entrance. It was massive. I whimpered. "You are too big."

"We will manage. You are used regular, I can get the feel of that. You will take it. Your body will open right up to it. It wants the cock. The gut knows what it wants and will do what is needed. We were meant to dance this dance."

His fingers were still stretching me open as much as they could as, grunting, he moved his bulb inside me. I was panting heavily, and groaning and close to tears. It had been nothing like this with the men in the gym. None of them were built like this English farmer. None of them were as forceful or determined. None of them had the gall to tell me what I wanted. I had told him he was too big. He hadn't seen it as a problem.

But, he was right. I wanted it so much. "Ahhhhhhhhh."

"Arch back from me," he commanded. His voice was demanding, like he was trying to override my approach toward hyperventilating. "Don't worry; I will hold you."

He was so powerful and his rough hands were so broad and strong, that I believed him.

"It will roll your pelvis up to me. The angle will be better, the channel straighter for the cock." He crouched a bit again, ready to maintain our balance by offsetting the arching of my torso. Again, the straightforward, confident, bald talk of the rudimentary elements of the fuck. Again, too, the understanding of the basic mechanics of it. Almost clinical. He just wanted to get deep inside me, to come inside me. Get his rocks off and get back to the fields. A barnyard breeding. The farm stud.

But he *was* a stud.

I wanted him inside me as much as he wanted to be there. I was crazy to be doing this. I couldn't take a cock this big—and wouldn't enjoy it if I did. But, god, I wanted him deep inside me. None of what I wanted mattered now, though, he was going to fuck me. He was exuding no doubt. To him it was all mechanics; just a day on the farm, studding the livestock. A bit of pleasure in the process. His pleasure.

I arched back, afraid that I might fall back, but he smoothly counterbalanced with his crouch and I managed to grip his upper arms—massively muscular, making me melt to him even in the heat of trying to sheath his cock, and he was still holding my lower body close to his with the strength of his hands gripping my buttocks.

"I can support you. The cock wants this angle."

"Please, please, pleaseplease," I chanted in a faraway voice as, my prayer being answered, I felt his cock sliding slowly inside me, stretching and filling me. Knowing every inch of me inside as it sank into me; knowing too that the channel would expand to accommodate, to welcome the long slide. Making me pant and groan and moan. He was inside me. He was inside me! I wanted to shout for joy. I was taking him. It was throbbing inside me. Waiting, poised.

"There, the gut knows what it will take. A good angle and straight channel. Fully saddled. We can dance the fuck now." Like he was talking to some vet inseminating his prize brood mare.

I felt the fingers sliding out of me, their work finished. His hands went to my waist.

"Lift the other leg. Lock your ankles behind my back."

"Please. Please."

"What?"

"Please be patient with me. Please don't ruin me. It . . . is . . . so . . . big."

It was idiotic. I didn't know what I wanted by saying this at this point. I already was holed. But, yes, yes, I did. I wanted some sign from him before he started what came next that this was lovemaking, not just breeding, not just the primeval need to ejaculate. That he wanted me because he was attracted to me, not just because I had a channel and he wanted his huge cock sheathed tonight, just wanted a vessel to spill his seed in, had to get his rocks off. Throwing in my face that I had come onto him. Leaving me no shred of belief that I controlled . . . anything.

But then, what if he did? What if he only wanted his pleasure? The offer of the cottage had been clear enough. He was being completely honest. And I couldn't deny that he was giving me what I hoped to find here.

Thoughts of my own behavior, back in New York, floated through my brain. Isn't the way he was treating me no more impersonal than I treated those men in the gym? Letting them fuck me just to help push me beyond a blockage in my writing. I told them what they could do, how they could do it. Using them just like this self-confident farmer was going to use me, was already using me. Was I any more thoughtful of their needs than he was of mine?

"You came to me for the hard cocking. I see nothing innocent in you. Your gut speaks for what you want. The looseness of the gut tells me what you'll take."

No mercy to be had. What could I say to that? He was absolutely right.

He laughed a low laugh. "We will dance well together. Before the night is through, we will fit perfectly. Raise your other leg, or I will raise it for you. The cock wants it."

I let out a low sob and raised my leg. I also started to raise my torso to him.

"No, stay arched back. The angle is good. The angle is good for you, is it not? I am in deep, no? You feel me deep inside? It will be a long, straight stroke. The cock wants a long stroke."

The cock wants this; the cock wants that. What about what I want? But I knew what I wanted. I wanted the cock.

"You're so big, so deep," I murmured. It came out with another low sob, but also with a sense that he was concerned for my pleasure after all, if only a little. I needed more from him. "No man has ever been that deep. You are magnificent."

Pimping for some sign of passion for me.

Nothing. But perhaps the intensity with which he was concentrating on the fuck should give me an indication how much he wanted it.

"Good. It's a good angle for me. I can stroke deep, long. Listen to the music. Feel the beat. This is the Dance of Life sonata. This movement is the primeval Dance of the Fuck." He laughed and I didn't know whether to take him seriously or not. His terminology was idiotic. It was just a fuck. But this was not a moment to give it any thought. "We will dance now, you and I. The Dance of the Fuck."

And then he began to pump me, pulling me back and forth on his cock, leveraging me with those beefy hands on my waist. He must have timed this with the music he knew was coming, because as the beat increased in the music and became louder and louder, his pumping kept up with the beat, fucking faster and deeper and harder. Pulling me further out now. Slamming me back down on the cock harder each time. He was shuffling his feet too, dancing in place, groaning and grunting now. Getting his rocks off. I was crying out with each deep thrust. He didn't care. Eventually I was crying out *for* each deep thrust. He laughed.

"It is good for you. I knew you wanted it hard. Keep the angle. The deep stroke is good."

I was lost to him and the music. Writhing under his power, begging him to slow down, to stop for a rest, to speed up, to never stop. No indication he even was listening to me. Babbling and digging my fingernails into his upper arms, unable even to break the skin as thick and tightly stretched as the skin was over his muscles. He was indestructible, unstoppable, unflappable, Supercocker; I was whatever he wanted me to be. Just a tight sheath for his cock, a vessel for his primeval need to fuck. And overwhelmed by the beat of the music, the pumping of the cock.

He fucked me for an eternity. Long, hard, deep. The thought racing across my mind: just like the cock wanted it.

Just like I was loving it, like never before. He had known what I wanted after all.

I ejaculated again, and he laughed. Then he slowed down the pumping to where he was just standing there, rocking back and forth on his feet. The CD was changing to different music. Softer, less primeval.

"Oh, god . . . that . . . was . . . I don't know what to say."

"It's not finished yet. I haven't come."

Oh, shit.

He revolved me on his cock, instructing me what to do with my legs and arms, so that, still plastered to his pelvis, I was hanging off the front of him, facing away from him, my ankles hooked on the tops of his calves and my fists locked behind his neck, him half crouching to make my smallness accommodate to his height. The beat of the music started going faster again and pushing into the foreground, and, holding my waist in his hands, he was pumping me again . . . slamming my channel up and down on his cock, all glorious primeval brutality now . . . eventually to his own ejaculation.

We held there for the longest minute, both panting hard, both animals of the farm, having expended the red-hot, uncontrollable heat of doing what nature told us we must do.

"That was a good one."

Simply that. Good? That was stupendous. I had never been so fully fucked before.

I had visions of me on all fours, like a farmyard animal, and him covering me and fucking me like a dog or a sheep. A horse. Yes, a horse, with that horse cock of his. A stud bull. Treating me just like any other animal he possessed. No condom in this vision. Strongly shooting off inside me, flooding me with semen. Breeding me, seeding me. Drowning in his hot cum. Just another day on the farm. But me loving every thrust of him. My eyes darting around the farmyard, looking for, yearning for his approach. Going down on all fours for him. Raising my "arse" for the long, thick slide of him.

"We will dance on the bed."

"Oh, god. I don't know if I—"

"Not right away. But later. Now we both rest."

"I can't, again, tonight," I murmured as he let me down and helped me to hobble to the bed and lay down. He sat on the bed beside me, moving a hand over my chest and belly, going to my nipples to tweak them.

"You were good," he said. "The best in some time. We dance well together. You are well used. The gut opens as needed."

I melted. Despite the bald, rude language, he wanted me. Me. Not just my ass. He was still here. Why was I trying to send him away?

"Anyone ever compare you to a stud bull?" I asked. I think I meant that as an admonishment, a jab at his self-possessed doggedness, a teasing of how much he obviously thought of himself. The basic animalism of him was flooding my brain. A character was forming to intrude himself into my current book. Primitive, powerful, a stud bull, one who took what he wanted, when he wanted it. A prime breeder.

I wanted to get at the computer keyboard. And yet that was just my brain. That's not what my body was telling me I wanted.

"Yes, often," he said, with a smile, the possible criticism of it flying right over his head. "I am the best you will have here. We start again soon. I think I cock you better than you have had. I think you don't have a stud bull in America like me."

As arrogant as he was about it, I could not naysay him.

"I can't anymore tonight. It was . . . terrific. Well, more than terrific. Beyond my wildest dreams of what I could have here. But I work at night. I fuck for inspiration. I have inspiration for two novels after that . . . remarkable fuck."

"You are here for two weeks. You don't have to write on the first night. We will dance on the bed tonight—and maybe in the morning too, before I go to the fields, before dawn. You are one sexy piece."

"I . . ." He was stroking my cock. And my cock was appreciating the attention. I looked and saw that his cock was already engorging again as well. Magnificent. A horse. A stud bull. And he had been inside me—to the root. And I had taken it all.

"We will take this night for cocking." It wasn't a question.

I moaned and stretched out on the bed, turning on my back and flexing my muscles, working the kinks out from the demanding positions already taken. I almost felt like I was purring. I wondered if he could hear me purring. My pelvis was moving with his stroking of my cock. I willed it to stop, but it wouldn't. He made a circle of his fingers, and my cock was slowly, sensuously stroking in the sheath it provided—on its own accord.

"You want me again. Now. You ache to have my cock inside you again."

Had I, in fact, been purring and he had heard it? Why couldn't I control my cock?

The music on the CD that had been muted in the interim was growing noticeably in volume and beat.

"I really can't." Fighting for some shred of control—over myself as much as over him.

He came up on the bed, stretching himself beside me. The beat of the music was picking up. He managed to trap my wrists in the powerful grip of one hand and pulled them over my head. The other hand, palm up, was pressing between my thighs. My body lost all loyalty to my intentions. My legs, on their own, spread, my knees went up, my heels dug into the bedspread, and my pelvis rolled up to him as two beefy fingers entered my ass, found my prostate, started to rub.

"I think I could get the whole fist up here now."

I froze, panicked.

"But such a sweet arse is for the cock."

I relaxed, but only a bit. The rubbing of the fingers was sending me over the moon.

Yes, fuck me again. Deep and hard. You know what I like. Better than I do.

I hadn't said it out loud, had I? No, I don't think so. He hadn't responded.

I looked wildly up into his eyes. His face was smiling, his eyes were flashing the totality of his control, his intention. His assurance that it was what I wanted. Looking away, my gaze went down the length of his achingly beautiful muscular chest.

How had he managed to get another condom on? I had seen him take the other one off and toss it on the floor, mesmerized by how bloated it was with creamy cum. Remembering shivering at the thought of him barebacking me, breeding me, the explosive ejaculation deep inside me and the lathering of my channel with all that cum. Aching for his cum, his total possession of me. Oh, shit. There were two more packets on the bedspread.

My eyes went back to his face.

"The Dance of the Bed," he murmured.

I started to weakly, unconvincingly object again, but his lips were covering mine, his tongue pushing them apart and invading. The music was getting louder, the beat more demanding.

He was turning me on my side, his fingers out of my channel now. He was raising my leg with a firm grip. The bulb of his cock at my entrance.

YES!

Again, I hadn't actually screamed that, had I?

I broke from the kiss, arched my back, and howled to the thatched ceiling above our heads, as he slid into me again. "Oh, god, you are so big. Oh shit. So deep so fast."

This time, though, I found it wasn't an objection. It was glorious. He had been right. We were ideal dancing partners. Now he fit me perfectly. Reamed to fit him.

"See," he said, full of his rightness, "the gut has its measure now. You want it. You want it big. You don't have a stud bull in America. You came here for this cock. You came to my farm looking for a stud bull. And you found one. It's all good for you."

God knows he was right. For two weeks he'd be going to his fields, whistling, and I'd be laying here, moaning, and not being able to close my legs. And loving every thrust of it.

He began to rock against me, moving his cock inside me, not pumping yet. I moved my hips too, realizing that it was to the beat of the music.

The beginning of the Dance of the Bed.

"Open your gut to me," he growled. I grabbed my butt cheeks and spread them as much as I could, doing everything I could to respond to his demands.

On a String in Bangkok

In more recent years I look back on my mid-1970s (and then again early 1980s) Bangkok adventure and just shake my head, wondering what we were thinking we were doing then and how shallow we must have been to be so totally focused on beautiful bodies and the striving for perpetual orgasm.

I think that for most of those I played with for two-and-a-half years in the 1970s, the hedonist urges resulted from the intersection of a few "realities." As a society, Americans were coming out of a decade of national hedonism in the form of the flower child/hippie generation that, itself, lifted the orgasm and the concept of "if it gives pleasure, do it" to the level of both a desirable and an obtainable goal. Overlaying that was that we were just coming out of a physically and emotionally draining Vietnam War period in which we not only suffered the depression of defeat (no matter what a spin our government tried to put on it) but in which, like so many other wars, we had lost the cream of our generation—our very generation, those we had grown up with and had mistakenly assumed we would grow old with. The "pack all of the pleasure in today, because tomorrow we die" syndrome was laying heavy on us, especially on those of us in Thailand, close still to Saigon.

Add to that that Americans finding themselves living and working in Bangkok were basically adventuresome folks and that, with the jobs they did, they tended to be beautiful and fit folks, Bangkok was, morally, a wide-open, "if it feels good, do it" society. So we had a heady brew of an invitation to sexual adventure, openness, and experimentation. The horror of AIDS wasn't even a moat in anyone's eyes yet.

This mix was particularly heady for me. I came to Bangkok a vanilla monogamous heterosexual, who had had thoughts of a world further afield than heterosexuality, but who had been so narcissistic that I hadn't given more than a passing thought to sex at all outside of marriage let alone in pursuing the goal of perpetual orgasm with multiple partners, and those of the same gender as I was. All of that exploded early in my Bangkok diplomatic tour when, naïvely not even seeing what I was sinking into, I was seduced by a sexual magician male Indian doctor, who was an expert in the sexual positions of the Kamasutra, and whose goal it was to totally debauch, master, and control largely innocent young men—and to make them open to having multiple partners simultaneously.

Within months of arriving in Bangkok, I was attending male-only nude pool parties and laying on a chaise lounge by the pool, with my legs perpetually open to a parade of cocks—and not thinking a bit of anything but the pleasure of being wanted by beautiful men, one after the other, with hard, muscled bodies and a goal of the perpetual orgasm.

Particularly perplexing to me now, decades later, with all that has happened in my life and the trending of societal attitudes and medical reality, is how easy it was for me to accept the dripping cock of one man to be immediately replaced by the hopeful hardness of that of another one—as long as both men were beautiful and hardbodied and said they wanted me . . . extending sometimes to the third and the forth cock. The thought of life-threatening disease wasn't even an issue then, as AIDS was a reality for the future, not for that present. Ironically enough, I once again was living—and fucking indiscriminately—in Bangkok in the mid 1980s, when the reality of AIDS did thunder in—and it coldcocked much of the freewheeling rolling sex party atmosphere of the city's expatriate gay male community. But not at the time I am speaking of here, the mid-1970s.

When I look for explanations for my own behavior, I see my narcissism as a dominant factor—more than the physical pleasure of melding with a beautiful body, being closely embraced by hard muscle, and feeling a hard cock churning in my gut, the explosive release of my own building orgasm and the jerk and spout and flow of hot cum inside me, again and again. But what motivated me most was the emotional pleasure of knowing that someone worshipped my body and wanted to possess it fully, was willing to surrender their manliness and the control of their desires to the squeezing of my channel muscles. It was at the height of my partner's impassioned, uncontrolled drive that I felt the most powerful—when they couldn't stop even if they wanted to. This was why it was sometimes the rough, dominating sex that made me soar the highest—the man wanted me so badly he was lost in his primeval lustings. It wasn't him in control; it was me—and my beautiful body. Pure narcissism.

And the thrill of partners in quick succession? To see the look in the eyes of the man standing behind the man then plowing me—and to the man standing next to him—to see the want and impatience of them, the way they couldn't keep their hands off their own cocks and how hard their cocks were getting—in anticipation of me, of being inside me, of having their turn at doing to me what someone else was then doing. To see how they couldn't keep their eyes off me. The enjoyment of the assessing of their individual attributes, an unusually muscled chest here with prominent nipples, a riot-of-color tattoo there. A flaming red bush, ebony skin next to alabaster, unusually beefy hands, black, curly chest hair in an arousing pattern, a short but thick cock, an unusually long one, low-hanging balls the size of ping-pong balls, a crook on a cock that had me wondering whether it would be felt differently inside me, an "oh my god" thick cock ring. All of these observations, even while I was arching my back and the lover of the moment was thrusting, thrusting, thrusting hard inside me and sucking on my nipple, made the multiple partners, in succession, hot, and a desirable goal in the atmosphere of gay Bangkok in the mid-1970s.

There were only a few Caucasian men in the city who would go on a string—that's what we called taking one guy after another in a session. Mostly young Thai men did this—and usually effeminate ones. Thanks to the conditioning of the Indian doctor, I was an American who, under controlled circumstances, would do so. And most who flocked to me said they appreciated that I wasn't limp wristed and effecting the pretense of being female.

* * * *

Rodney—insisting to go by Rod—was a Marine guard at the embassy. I passed him there, standing guard in the embassy's foyer, a couple of times a week. But where I knew him from was as someone else who played tennis on Saturday mornings and afternoons with me, some other embassy men, and high-ranking Thai military officers at the Thai Military Academy compound adjacent to the American embassy complex on Wireless Road. We played in that venue as much for the business of diplomacy—the contact with high-ranking military officers in a nation that was having a military coup every two years or so—as much as the exercise. The exercise was good, though. The Bangkok climate is sweltering hot. We'd go through a couple of two-liter bottles of Coke each during the three or four hours we were at it. The fat would boil off of us and flow away in the sweat. Everyone who participated was hardbodied; most of them were beautiful to boot.

We played shirtless and in skimpy shorts. I liked the way Rod looked. He obviously liked the way I looked too, as he propositioned me. Pretty straightforward and bald about it, he was, which I learned was a trademark of his. He thought the world of himself, of his own looks, and he assumed everyone else did too. He was fucking one of the Thai colonels there. Neither of them made much of a secret of it. This was Bangkok in the mid-1970s. Thai men tended to be at least bi, taking their pleasures where they could get them. The colonel had propositioned me, too, but was disappointed to learn that I wanted my sex the same way he did. I didn't tell my embassy mentors of this proposition, as the colonel was so well positioned in the Thai military hierarchy that they would have wanted to me somehow accept his proposition and do what pleased him to establish the contact. My supervisors didn't mind my activities as long as they served their needs when they saw the need.

In fact, at length, my Saturday tennis activities became a professional duty for me and I did hook up with high-ranking Thai military officers who I could use while being used by hem.

I turned Rod down—politely. By then I was accustomed to the proposition. I'd gotten them before coming to Bangkok, where I had only slowly learned to identify them as such. After arriving in Bangkok, they came left and right and weren't usually disguised well in a conversation that could be gracefully exited. But at that point I had not yet been cornered in a gym sauna by the sensuous hands and mesmerizing voice of a crafty Indian doctor, taken home by him, turned on explosively to my latent desires, stripped of my male-on-male virginity, and fucked to ejaculation repeatedly in every position imaginable. Through his weeks of conditioning my defenses were worn down over multiple sessions to the point that he could bring in other men and I'd open my legs and roll up my pelvis for a succession of them in a single sex session.

Rod was a cute blond with a buzz cut. Only about five foot six, but all body-builder muscle. He had tattoos, the military ones the Marines liked before they banned tattoos altogether. And he strutted around like a bantam rooster. It was his lack of height, I think that is what made him so cocky; he was trying to compensate. That's sort of a type of U.S. Marine—guys of that type often try to join the Marines to compensate for size. And not just in height. That type tends to have small cocks too. In his case, he might have been not quite five inches long—but he was a good two inches thick. I knew that, because that was how he propositioned me that first time. We were taking a break under a straggly tree next to the tennis court, which accorded just about all the shade there was to have, and he just leaned over me, pushed the front of his shorts down to below his balls, and said. "Willy's hard for you. Let's go someplace after tennis today." And he *was* hard, but not impressively so.

That was his form of directness. He had assumed I was available, because in those days so many were. I just wasn't yet— at least not that week. I think his proposition, though, is what helped weaken me when the Indian doctor put his hand on my cock in a sauna a couple of weeks later, making me come for the first time with a man, and, showing me a much more impressive cock, cast a spell on me with his mesmerizing voice that drew me onto the examination table of his home office with its stirrups and cuffs—and its progressively more complex sexual experiences and demands to give up my every sexual inhibition.

The Marine, Rod, just blew it off when I politely told him I didn't swing that way. A couple of months later, though, when he was cruising the pool at an all-male nude pool party and saw me being fucked, he was a bit more miffed. The party was being thrown at the house of a U.S. Army officer working for JUSMAG, the U.S. military advisory group to the Thai military, who I knew because we were both involved in an expatriate theater group, as was Rod, who was a stage hand there. By this time, I had already been picked up by a big, black JUSMAG major, with a body-builder's physique and a monster cock. To this day, when I think of well fucked, my mind goes to my black major, and when Rod saw me that day, I was already fucking around, but I was a captive of this major's cock. One thing about the Indian doctor, his indoctrination program moved fast.

I was on my shoulder blades on a chaise lounge. The black major was standing, his legs straddling the sides of the lounger. He was gripping my butt cheeks in his hands and had pulled my pelvis up to his. My feet also were on the patio tiles next to the lounger and my body arched up to the black major, my feet rocking back and forth on the warm tiles to the rhythm of the fuck. His cock was stroking my channel in long, deep slides. (Thinking back on the teachings of the Indian doctor, I knew this to be a variation on the Kamasutra position of The Stem. I would have told the black major this, but I knew that he wanted to think that all of these positions were of his own invention.) And I was gazing up into his handsome face with

140

glazed eyes. A small group had gathered to watch a master cocker in action; most were pulling on their cocks. I wasn't turning my face to them very often, wondering who was next, though. There was no gang-banging following the major. He fucked for an hour or so and wanted at least two ejaculations—I would get more—before he stopped. There was never much left of me for anyone else after one of those sessions. I heard my name and looked up, into the angry eyes of Rod, the Marine. He just gave me a withering look, muttered, "Fuck you later," and walked off.

Later was after closing one evening the next week on a platform on the stage at the Bhirasri Institute, the facility that the expatriate theater group used for its plays.

For Rod, a fuck was all about him. I let him fuck me that first time out of curiosity, a sense of "what the hell, it's just a fuck" attitude that was prominent in Bangkok in that period, and because I saw nothing good in having one of the embassy's Marine guards angry at me.

"Yes your hole can take it. I'm not too thick for you if you want to take it—and you *will* take it, because you're not leaving here until you do. Move here, like this. Willy wants this angle."

Of course my hole can take it, jackass, I thought. The major is just as thick as you are—a hell of a lot longer too. And do you see me running for the exits at the sight of your short little "Willy"? Who got you to calling it that juvenile name anyway?

"Willy" wanted to take fast, shallow, rabbit-punch strokes just to the prostate. (So, who cared what my channel wanted?) His cocking was like a jackhammer. He had power, I'll give him that, and as long as he was making it to the prostate, I wasn't going to complain. He held my legs up and together with fists grabbing my ankles while he fucked me missionary style. I'm sure he held my legs together to tighten my hole and accentuate the effect inside me of his thick cock. No working me with his hands, which were imprisoning my ankles. He was looking down at the jabbing of his cock in my entrance, very pleased with the job he was doing. Everything was concentrated on the pleasure of his cock—and of his image of himself. He fit

141

the description of a bantam rooster perfectly. Arrogant little bastard.

I'll admit, though that, for variety, I liked his cocking—that and as long as the body was hard and well muscled, they could take me any way they wanted to. He was body-builder hard. Not many pistoned hard like a jackrabbit to a depth of just four inches or so (although I have seen that since in porn videos occasionally). I think being only a bit longer than that four inches, he liked the sensation of not all of his cock being able to go into the hole—like he could pretend it was a mammoth length or something.

No pretty talk once he got started. All business of what pleased him. Taking what he wanted with a thick cock and a beautiful body as if by right, ejaculating in great globs of cum near the surface (condoms were considered sissy in those days), and just pulling out and strutting away, whether or not I'd come, leaving me panting, with my legs flopping open to the sides. It was all over in seven or eight minutes. I hadn't come. He didn't give a shit whether I came or not.

The first time, I thought he didn't like the fuck. But the next night, after theater practice, he wanted it again. Just like the first time.

"Move your ass to this position; role your hips up more; it's a good angle for Willy."

And he kept pestering me thereafter. It was no big deal saying yes. I let all of the male actors and stage hands who wanted to but who weren't exclusive bottoms themselves fuck me—as did most of the others with each other. In his case, though, I savored the victory of him doing the asking for sex. I never begged it from him; his body was good but the cocking was nothing special. And it was I, not him, with ultimate control after that first time. Knowing he was going to come quickly and then leave, I wouldn't go with him again unless he embraced me closely with his muscled body with his fingers moving inside my passage until I had jacked myself off. Only then could he fuck me. He refused to suck me or to do the jacking himself. He actually seemed to like fingering me while I jacked off (since he continued to ask me for it). His ejaculation then legitimately was the closing curtain. I think he was self-conscious about being a

142

fast ejaculator. As far as I know, he didn't rebuild fast, so that one time was what there was going to be—but he produced enough cum for three times. As a Marine, I think he saw his size and lack of stamina as substandard.

Did his length matter to me? Certainly not as much as it seemed to matter to him. The size of a cock only mattered to me if it was extraordinarily long—and then more if it also was thick. Other than that, it didn't matter to me at all. And I wasn't moved by the physicality of the length and thickness, really, as much as by the emotional sense that something that size was possessing me—and that I was taking it all. If a huge cock just jabbed four inches inside me like Rod's did, its size meant nothing to me. When a guy had a long cock, I insisted on taking it all inside me.

When the length mattered, it was because I could feel it deep inside me, and I could feel my bush mingling with his, knowing he had put it all inside me—that's when I had the emotional high of being totally taken. The black major did that for me. He was both extraordinarily long and thick, and he fucked me deep. And he knew I soared to the feel of the depth of him inside me. Bush would entwine with bush, and he'd loosen his embrace of me and let my torso relax back with his arm supporting the small of my back, me panting, and literally purring, letting my arms just dangle down onto the mattress and my head flop back, all of my senses going to my gut. He'd hold for a full minute, maybe more, letting the pleasure of him deep inside me roll over me in waves. And then he would start short stroking, deep, and I would start to moan and jabber, and he'd pull me back to his chest and move into the long, deep stroking. This was heaven if the cock was long and thick. And any bottom who doesn't say they prefer it this way is, I think, full of crap.

Of course I'd tell any man I was with, who wasn't obviously small, that he was deep inside me. I've never met a man who didn't want to hear that. If he was small, I just made sure he knew how to reach my prostate, and then I'd please him by shuddering at him working that and clutching him close to me. He had to be well muscled, though. Skinny or heavy only worked when the cock was oversized and he knew how to use it to best advantage.

The Indian doctor wasn't thick, but he was among the longest I've had, and his cock was evil. His cock had the flexibility of a snake. I felt he could almost reach my stomach with it, but it was the other things it did inside me that had me charmed and kept me coming to the Indian doctor—and *for* the Indian doctor—long after I knew that his hold over me was evil. He could slap my channel walls with it or caress them as my moaning directed him, or revolve it inside me so that it rubbed against the channel walls in revolving succession, and he could make me come just with the sensation that the head of it was latched onto my prostate and sucking it hard. Now, after all these years, I think he was drugging the drinks he gave me before we fucked and that, with me in a mild hallucinatory state, he was whispering in my ear what his cock was doing inside me, and I was taking that for reality. Whatever the circumstance, he had me in thrall, until he released me for some reason, a magnet for men who wanted other men and conditioned to be an easy slut, into a hedonist city.

The bantam rooster, cocksure Marine guard, Rodney, was reassigned from Bangkok a couple of months after he started with me. I didn't miss him.

* * * *

What the first time that the Marine fucked me on my back on a platform on the Bhirasri stage provides in connection with the multiple partner theme of this remembrance is what happened after he pulled out of me and just strutted off, leaving me uncompleted.

The Marine had just left me, flopped out on my back all askew, panting, and my legs spread open from the release of his ankle hold, buzzed by the pistoning of a thick cock inside the entrance of a tightened hole and by the three strong spurts of his cum up into my channel—but not completed myself. Within seconds, a tall Thai guy I never saw again and who likely had been watching, and stripped while he did so, slipped in from the shadows and finished me with a long cock squishing through the still-warm cum the Marine left inside me. A thin, lithe, berry-brown body—good muscle tone, though, which most Thai men

144

have because they are manual laborers—torso covered with blue tribal tattoos. The proverbial Thai smile of "everything's just fine; you'll like this." And I did.

He whispered to me in Thai—maybe asking for permission, maybe telling me he couldn't resist, maybe admonishing me for being a slut and telling me I needed to be punished. I don't know what he said; unfortunately I didn't speak Thai. As long as he was going to finish me—and do a good job of it—I didn't care. He showed every indication that's what he was going to do. Whatever he had said didn't prevent him from gently taking hold of my ankles again, raising and spreading my legs, and taking a long, long slide into me that had me arching my back and burbling my pleasure and acceptance of a second cock within barely a minute.

He smiled, knowing by how I groaned and clutched his waist with my hands, holding him to me, that I wanted him inside me.

Long, slow, deep strokes, me coming first—and second—but not right away, and him later, deep inside—again, condoms weren't thought necessary there yet, and fuck strings were fairly common, more than one guy in succession. He fucked me longer than the Marine had—some half an hour of "this is what a fuck should be." He released my legs and let me dig my heels into the wood surface of the platform and raise my pelvis to him for an even deeper reach of the cock. He ran his hands over my torso and gave me nipple play. He even let me suck on his thumb while he slow-stroked me. The minutes clicked by. He stroked my cock, making me hard again—for him. But it was about both of us, not just him. He playing my body with his hands and his cock. He raised my pelvis to his face, palming my buttocks, taking my cock in his mouth and sucking me to a second ejaculation.

He lowered my pelvis and slid into me again, still hard, still long, still making me moan with pleasure.

Maybe what he had said at the beginning was, "Sorry about that little bastard. Let me show you how it's done." Because he was doing a great job of showing how it's done well.

He squeezed my knees with his hands and moved them in and out with the rhythm of the stroke like I first experienced with the Indian doctor. That was pretty much a Bangkok technique that I haven't encountered much since then. I found it arousing, and in later years I asked my Lebanese lovers to do it—I would work my pelvis to the rhythm too. In the circumstances, I thought that was hot—even with him just pulling out and melting into the shadows again after ejaculating, retrieving some cum from inside me, and, giving me a smile, taking it to his lips.

I thought I'd see him again—and maybe experience him again—but I never did. He knew how to give and receive pleasure in a fuck. I occasionally thought about the encounter for months thereafter—until other memorable fucks caused it to recede into the recesses of my brain to only recently resurface by way of having my memory jogged by photographs.

Did I think twice at the time about letting a Thai stranger come in for a second fuck on the stage of an otherwise deserted theater? No, I didn't. What I thought about was wanting to have him inside me again. Would I do this today at that age, knowing what I know now—both the Marine and the Thai stranger (I won't even begin to think about the Indian doctor)? The Marine maybe—with a condom. The Thai stranger, probably not. Multiple partners in a string? Probably not that either.

But those were hedonist days in Bangkok, and, who knows, perhaps they still are today. A friend recently sent me a link to Internet pictures of the Bhirasri Institute in Bangkok—the photographs mentioned above. It was an art gallery as well as a theater. It's now unused, blocked off with a chain-link fence and derelict, covered with trash. I looked at current satellite photographs of Bangkok and found that the compound with the pool where the JUSMAG officer held those male-only nude pool parties is now the location of a high-rise hotel (with, perhaps, just as much sex going on in its rooms as went on at that pool on a Sunday afternoon).

I wonder who is fucking who in Bangkok today, where, and with how many partners?

Training Asu

"You cannot put it off any longer, my friend. If you do not choose for Asu soon, the priests will take him. The choice will no longer be yours—or Asu's. He is of age for starting the life chosen for him. He cannot do other than meet his destiny."

"I know that, Sargon, it is just so hard . . ."

Baltasar, the wood merchant, was sitting at a table outside of the tea shop in the bazaar, sipping a blend that the owner of the shop, Sargon, had recently received from the East and had invited his friend to try. Sargon had, in fact, been pestering him to stop by, but Baltasar had been keeping to his own apartments above his shop for some time—precisely because he didn't want to have this conversation with anyone.

"You know what Asu is meant for, Baltasar. You've known for years. His destiny for it has been evident since he was a child. He knows too, I am sure. He has not tried to leave the city, as some others have under these circumstances—until they are dragged back. So he is resigned to it."

"Yes, yes. All of that is true. But it's hard . . ."

"I could recommend the perfect place for him. There is a wine shop just inside the bazaar on the high road, almost in the shadow of the palace. That would be perfect for him. The wealthiest merchants and even the king's officers go there. He would be your family's fortunes."

And yet Baltasar hesitated.

"It is inevitable. He is of age. The priests would do the same with him. Why not secure the family's fortune rather than just having some meaningless tablet of favor from the temple to hang on your shop wall?"

After a brief pause. "You know of this wine shop? Do you really think it is the best opportunity for him?"

"I go there myself."

* * * *

"Do not wiggle away from the patrons like that," the wine shop owner, Hatim, hissed at Asu as he took him aside at the end of the long table the wine was served from. A soldier of the Palace Guard, Nasri, was leaning on the end of the table, several cups of wine into his evening. He, like all of the palace guardsmen, was a massive, heavily muscled man, battle forged. His chest and arm and thigh muscles were bulging. Clearly discernible as a mark of the elite palace soldiers was his short, heavy-leather slab skirt, sandals laced up to his knees, a chest medallion declaring his rank, and nothing else. The merchants and other private citizens of the town wore long gowns, called thawbs, of various quality of material. Most worn on the street were white in color.

"Sorry, master," Asu whispered back. "It is just so difficult."

"Do you want to be here, performing as required, or shall I take you to the priests at the temple myself?"

Hatim held his breath for the answer to that. Asu was far too beautiful for Hatim to want to lose him at the shop—and just as he and the tea shop owner, Sargon, had discussed, it would be one of the world's tragedies to see Asu taken into the temple, not to be seen again, even if then, until after his beauty had been wiped away by continuous sacrifices to the gods.

The youth was small, but perfectly formed, with curly black hair and a sensuous smile. It was hard to believe he was of age, but everyone in the bazaar knew of everyone else's age. They had all watched Asu grow to adulthood—some watched more closely and with much greater interest than others. Some with flashing eyes and licking lips and members that would harden under their thawbs as Asu walked by.

There was no hiding that it was time for Asu. Everyone knew it. Therefore the ravenous priests knew it as well. The giving of Asu to the wine shop by his father, Baltasar, estopped the certain plans of the priests, but for how long? If Asu could not cross over that curtain here willingly, the priests would take him and force him across the barrier. Asu knew that.

And Asu had just now traded his short cotton skirt, which, as he grew older and formed into perfection, drove many in the bazaar to distraction, for the thawb. The thawb could hide his form, but it could not hide his beauty. The priests will have noticed by now that the changing ceremony—the change from a short skirt to a thawb—that marked for all to see the cross to adulthood had been performed.

"I know, I know," Asu said, a slight edge of panic in his voice. "Just be patient with me, please. It's such a hard curtain to cross."

"Try faster," Hatim hissed. "See your sponsor over there. His cup is empty and he is showing its emptiness to you. He's a rich and powerful man. Take him this cup of wine—and do as he wishes."

Asu was trembling as he came around from behind the wine table. He was watching the nearly full cup he was carrying, trying hard not to spill any of the wine, his mind racing on this trip he was making—just across the wine shop floor, but perhaps across the curtain as well. As he passed around the side of the table, the burly soldier, Nasri, grabbed one of Asu's rounded buttocks cheek through the material of his white cotton thawb, and Asu nearly spilled the wine. When he looked into Nasri's face, the soldier winked and leered at him.

Asu scurried over to the table Hatim had directed him to.

"Put the wine cup down," Asu's father's friend, Sargon, said in an alcohol slurred voice, low and husky. "And come, into my lap, and feel what a man is like."

149

The tea shop owner pulled Asu roughly down into his lap and held him close to him in the embrace of an arm slung across Asu's little chest. Sargon was big and fat but his grip was strong. And his demanding lust was obvious. As Asu was pulled into Sargon's lap, he could feel the strength of a hard cock poking at his virginal buttocks.

"I have waited for years for this little one," Sargon growled. "Feel what I have for you?"

Indeed, Asu could feel it. Although he would normally wear a loin cloth under his thawb, Hatim had told him not to wear it in the wine shop. The shop owner had made no secret why that was so, and Asu had not needed to wonder why. The wine shops were brothels as well, and this one was a male brothel. The patrons did not come here only for the wine. The fate of each of the citizens of this city was sealed long before they reached adulthood. It depended on their family status and business—and in the case of the soldiers on their size and musculature and promise of fighting skills. For young men as small and beautiful and as well formed as Asu, their destinies were set for either a wine shop such as this or the priesthood, where their bodies would be used just as fully—and perhaps more brutally and more often. They just wouldn't receive the recompense that a wine shop gave, and the life span of a temple serving boy was sometimes marked in months, rather than years.

Sargon obviously wasn't wearing anything under his thawb either. Asu squirmed around on his lap—not being unwilling or railing against his fate, but being scared and needing more patience than he was being given. Sargon was fat and gross and smelled not just of the wine, but also of the opiate he smoked and the spices he was served in his food that few others in the city could afford. And he was being rough and brutal. With his free hand, he reached around and grabbed Asu's balls through the material of the thawb, and squeezed.

"Don't fight. Or do fight me, it will make the taking all that more pleasurable. I will have you here and now. I have waited and schemed for too long."

Asu, eyes watering, looked toward the wine table in panic. Hatim and the solider, Nasri, had their heads together in quiet conversation and were watching him.

Sargon was moving Asu's rump around on his cock, almost, but not quite, achieving penetration through the two layers of cloth. His hand stopped squeezing Asu's balls, but only so that it could gather up the hem of Asu's thawb and work its way onto Asu's leg. His long fingernails were scraping their way up the inside of Asu's thigh.

The young man wailed, "Not yet . . . please," and managed to break away from Sargon and almost stumble out onto the floor beside the table. He did go down on his knee, but while Sargon roared his anger behind him, Asu found his footing and struggled, the other men now in the hunt, each wanting to be the first, snatching at him with their hands as he passed.

He was nearly sobbing when he reached the relative safety behind the bar table again.

Surprisingly, Hatim didn't admonish him. Rather, he held out a cup of wine and said, "Here, calm yourself, Asu. Drink this to calm yourself."

Asu downed the cup of wine. Wine was not something that you were permitted to have before you came of age. Thus, although Asu had had a bit now and then and more than a bit in the week since his ceremony of change, this wine was stronger than he was accustomed to. So was the second cup.

He was feeling a bit woozy when he felt one of the soldier, Nasri's, hands on his arm and the other one on his waist. Asu looked, with unfocusing gaze, at the soldier's face. His expression was inscrutable. He was looking stern, but Asu noted a hint of a smile—and something else. The same lust that had been in Sargon's eyes.

As for Sargon, he was still loudly mouthing his indignation at his table, but was soon stopped as Hatim hovered at his table, another one of the serving boys beside him, Hatim's hand gripping the young man's wrist. Asu saw Sargon lifting the hem of his thawb to his belly, and Asu saw the plump, hard cock of the man. And then Asu watched the ass of the other serving boy descend on the cock. It was all unreeling like it was in a surreal dream, though.

"Your master is done with you," Nasri said in a growl. "I am taking you home."

"No," Asu whined. "He must give me another chance."

151

"You will come with me," Nasri said.

And there was no arguing with that, as Nasri had merely leaned over, taken Asu by the waist, and flung him over his shoulder.

Outside, after barely twenty steps, Asu was aware enough to say, "This is not the way to the wool merchant's quarter. This is not the way to my father's house."

Nasri reached up and slapped Asu on the rump and said, "Perhaps we are not going there. Perhaps I am taking you to the temple for the priests to debauch." And then he gave a hearty laugh.

* * * *

Supper couches, with gently raised backs, were fanned around the stone walls of the room. The floor was stone. So was the ceiling. There were torches, only half of them lit, fixed to the walls around the four sides. All of these couches were facing one, in the center of the room, that was flat.

The center couch had red-leather ropes attached to each of the four corners. The two at one end were tying off the wrists of a young man, swarthy in complexion, with a short beard and black body hair. The young man, not much taller than Asu, but more heavily muscled, covered in blue-tinted tattoos of primitive symbols, and thin of waist, with flaring thighs, and bulbous buttocks cheeks, was supporting the weight of his torso on his shoulder blades. His belly was inclined up, his jet-black cock and his heavy balls flopping back and forth, his black bush mingling with the more reddish, auburn bush of the man holding his torso on the incline and, kneeling between the darker-skinned man's thighs, grabbing his waist, and fucking him in hard thrusts.

One of the dark-skinned man's arms appeared to be broken—he screamed each time the thrust of the cock of his assailant jerked it. There were bloodied slashes across his chest and his thighs, and a dirty rag tied around one of his ankles. He was bleeding from a knife wound in his side. His knees were bent and lacerated—Nasri remarked to Asu that this was caused by sinking to them in defeat on the battlefield—and his bare feet, his ankles bound to the long, red cords at the foot of the

152

couch, were flat on the surface of the lounge on either side of the soldier's beefy thighs.

It was obvious that it was a member of the Palace Guard who was fucking him. The short skirt with the leather slabs was on the floor next to the couch, the soldier's sandals next to that, and the medallion of rank was still around the soldier's neck, swinging back and forth in rhythm with the thrusts of his cock. The soldier's musculature was magnificent, as it was with all of the palace guardsmen, and his cock was thick and was pistoning hard and fast.

The man tied to the couch had been screaming when Nasri carried Asu into the room over his shoulder. They had not gone to Asu's father's house, but they had not gone in the direction of the temple, either. The solider had carried Asu into the entrance of the king's palace and turned immediately to the right, entering the guard house and proceeding through that to the living quarters of the Palace Guard.

The man on the couch had long, black hair, in ringlets, and as Nasri and Asu entered the chamber, hearing the man's screams from as far away as the entrance into the palace forecourt, the soldier fucking him had grabbed him by the hair, punched him in the face with a fist, and pounded his head against the hard surface of the couch until the man was reduced to moans and groans.

The soldier grabbed the man's legs by the ankles and wishboned him in a wide, high spread to the limits that the red cords binding his ankles would permit, and started fucking his hole with deeper, anger-filled stabbing thrusts.

Upon entering the chamber, Nasri stopped about five paces from the center couch, pulled Asu down the front of his body, and held Asu to his pelvis. Still dazed, Asu had no trouble discerning that Nasri's cock pressing in the cleavage of his buttocks was harder and bigger than Sargon's had been.

Nasri pulled Asu's thawb over his head and cast it aside on the floor. All Asu was wearing now were his sandals and the golden chain around his neck that his father had given him for good luck.

"Hatim has paid me to get you over your reluctance," Nasri said. Both he and Asu had their eyes trained on the taking on the couch. "He wants it done fast and completely, and he wants you returned fully conditioned and resigned to it. Are you going to fight me?"

"No, Sire," Asu murmured. "I want it done as much as he does." His voice, however, revealed the great fear and regret with which he spoke this accepted truth.

"A pity perhaps," Nasri said. "I like an attempt to fight. That man on the couch has fought. But he has lost. A captive from battle yesterday out on the plains. Karan there saw a friend of his lose his life to this man in battle. The captive was given to Karan. I thought that Karan would be finished with him by now, but he is toying with him. He had started when I left for the wine shop. I thought the taking couch would be free. No matter, though, I will initiate you standing here while we watch."

Asu moaned and trembled in Nasri's embrace. Nasri was holding the shorter young man off the floor, with just one arm encircling his waist. Asu's body was jutting out from his at the pelvis, and his arms were dangling beside him. His head was lifted, though, and he was watching the brutal fucking on the couch. The soldier was up on his feet, crouching, taking deep, slamming thrusts into the captive's channel. Rearing his buttocks back to where the long, thick cock came out of the hole, and then ramming it inside with a hard thrust of his hips. The captive was groaning quietly, just hanging there, supported only by the soldier's hands on his waist raising the man's pelvis to the punishing cock. The wounds on his chest, side, and thighs had opened and blood was oozing out of them. There also was a trickle of blood coming down from his scalp in front and his lower lip and an ear, torn where the soldier must have taken bites out of him. Cum was dribbling out of his hole. There had been several takings. The soldier had even taken time out for refreshment and then come back to resume the attack.

Asu felt the leather skirt of his own soldier hit the floor and get pushed aside with a foot. And he felt the hard cylinder of the cock, skin on skin. Long, hard, thick. Another Palace Guard requirement. Virility was the pride of the city. When the guardsmen marched on parade in the city, they marched naked except for their medallions of rank. If they could not take pride in what was swinging between their thighs, they would not be in

154

the Palace Guard. Nasri's cock was lodged between Asu's thighs, pushing at the base of his balls and cock. He was slowing stroking, dry fucking Asu already.

"You are so big," Asu murmured in fright.

"The best to initiate you. When you can take the cock of a palace guardsmen, you will have no trouble in the wine shop. This is best for you. Tonight you will take more than one palace guardsman's cock. I promised to return you fully prepared."

Asu moaned and began to shudder.

"Do not fear, my sweet little one. I will take good care of you. I almost would not take Hatim's money. To be the first in one like you—to ream you to Palace Guard requirements—is reward enough in itself."

Over the next several moments, Nasri worked to get his cock inside Asu's hole, but it just wasn't working. Nasri was too big and Asu too virginal. Nasri gave up on the direct approach. He carried Asu over to one of the other couches, crouching down as he moved and retrieving the leather bands used as belting for his leather skirt. Laying Asu's back on the end of the couch, he called out, "Bring me taking grease."

In short order a Nubian slave arrived with the requested lotion. In the meantime Nasri had tied Asu's ankles together, pushed his legs up to his chest, and then tied his wrists in front of him, so that his legs were encased between his chest and his bound arms. When the slave arrived, Nasri was tonguing Asu's hole and patting it, commanding it to open for him.

Asu was moaning at the unexpected pleasure of this sensation. He arched his back and groaned loudly, though, when Nasri's beefy, greased fingers started to work at opening his channel up.

"Sorry that you must be bound," Nasri whispered. "But this must happen, and quickly. There will be no running away from me as you did from that fat, rich merchant, Sargon. Hatim has declared that when you come back you will sit on Sargon's cock—or not come back alive."

Asu moaned as much for what Nasri had said as for what he was doing with his fingers.

"Servants," a voice rang out from the center couch. "I think it is finished for now. I wouldn't want to use him up in one session. Come clean up and throw him in the cells."

Asu heard a scurrying of feet, the sound of something being carried off, scrubbing of the center couch and the floor around it—and then silence.

"Ah, good," he heard Nasri say. "We can use the taking couch after all."

Bound at all four corners of the couch, but with enough give that he could kneel on all fours, Asu had his head raised and his mouth hanging open, panting heavily and whimpering. Nasri was covering him close from above and slow pumping his cock inside Asu.

The screaming and begging for mercy were over—had been over for nearly half an hour. It had been difficult even with the taking grease and the preparation by the fingers, but Nasri was insistent and determined—and Asu was bound and helpless. Asu could take no more of the demands on his knees and elbows and, with a groan, he sank to the surface of the couch.

"Just as well," Nasri muttered. "I must ensure full access."

Asu had no idea what the soldier meant until he felt the giant pull out of him and the leather strips being secured around his thighs and his calves, holding his legs close together. He arched his back and screamed again as Nasri started working his cock into the now-tightened channel.

There had been a change of shift in the palace guardsmen, and those going off duty had passed those coming on duty in the supper room. The city was large, but the repute of Asu for beauty and the end of the counting of his days for the change ceremony were well known, so all stopped beside the center couch while passing from and to their duty. They could not believe their good fortune, when Nasri told them what he was doing with Asu, why, and that they all might have a part in it.

"We are preparing him for his wine shop duties, training him to take the cocks of men," Nasri told all who asked. "If you wish, those of you coming off duty, stay and you may have him too. And for those who are going on duty, we will still be here when you are relieved. But he is not for rough taking, lads. We are conditioning and hardening him, not punishing him. Keep that in mind, as hard it is, I know, for you not to be rough. I'm sure that all of you, like me, want to have him survive for our visits to Hatim's wine shop. He is our guest tonight, not our captive. The bindings are for his benefit."

Nasri came this time inside Asu. Asu had already come countless times in nervousness, fear, shock, and, eventually, the glory of the taking. As Nasri untied the leather strips around Asu's thighs and calves, another strapping, young palace guardsman stepped forward.

"Retie him on his back; just the arms," he said. Nearly a dozen hands moved quickly to untie Asu's wrists and ankles from the red cords; turn him, groaning; onto his back; and then rebinding his wrists to the corners of the couch. Taking a plump pillow from another couch, the strapping soldier climbed up onto the center couch with his knees, pushed the pillow under the small of Asu's back, wishboned his legs with fists grabbing his ankles, and slid a throbbing, hard cock inside him, easily opening a channel that had already been stretched by Nasri.

Asu could feel the difference of the cock, which surprised him, and although he cried out at the first thrust, this one wasn't as thick as Nasri was, so Asu felt prepared to take him. He also was younger than the rest and over anxious. Four thrusts and he exploded, adding his semen to that already contributed by Nasri.

"The gods be cursed," he cried out.

"No tragedy," Nasri said. "There is room at the end of this line."

The third man was content with taking Asu the same way, but subsequent guardsmen each had his own characteristics and preferences and feel. One even had Asu rebound with his knees pulled into his chest and ankles tied to wrists, laid him on his side on the couch, stood next to him, and plowed him sideways. Once taken across the curtain, Asu was grateful for this education—although the lessons could have stopped several hours before they did.

Mercifully, he was not there for the next change in shift. The captain of the guard strutted in on the proceedings, asked

157

the gathered guardsmen what in Hades were they doing with this young civilian of the city. When he was told, he ordered them to unbind the young man. Then he reached down and picked Asu up, threw the spent youth over his shoulder much as Nasri had done much earlier in the evening, and took Asu to his own, private quarters.

* * * *

The captain of the king's Palace Guard, Mahir, was not of the world of the subordinate guardmen's supper couches, or of the city's wine shops, or even of the city's merchant world. He was a senior official of the king and was a man of the palace court. His was not of a world of fucking serving boys in the wine shops; his was of the world of courtesans and of taking young men fully and well on silken couches and leaving them both sobbing and sighing, unable to close their legs and not wanting to, grasping at him for another throw.

Asu was trembling and moaning, hiccupping and groaning as the captain carried him into his bedchamber. The contrast between Mahir's quarters and those of the palace guardsmen was startling. Within the same stark stone walls that held the guardsmen's supper room, a luxurious chamber had been assembled—tapestries on the walls, carpets from the Orient on the floor, leather-seated campaign chairs, a large sleeping couch, covered by the skins of exotic wild animals, and a many-armed chandelier in the ceiling, casting bright light from a hundred candles.

A young man of handsome visage and dressed only in bangles and rouged nipples lay on the couch when Mahir entered, carrying Asu over his shoulder. Mahir waved away the courtesan, and when he, pouting, had removed himself, Mahir pulled Asu down to in front of his body, with Asu facing the bed. He encircled Asu's heaving belly with a strong arm, covered the young man's privates with a beefy hand, and let his hardening cock part Asu's thighs, the bulb pressing against the base of Asu's ball sac, giving Asu the sensation of his torso resting on a gigantic, throbbing cylinder. Asu knew what it was, though, and he panted in fearful anticipation.

The contrast in living styles was not the end of it. Mahir's body was unlike those of the younger Palace Guard soldiers, as well. To their Apollo physiques, he was a Zeus. Massive, barrel chested, and thick waisted, but all hard muscle, his cut torso the model for the shaped body plates the soldiers wore into battle. His thighs were as the trunks of the cedars and his feet and hands were broad and long, with long, plump digits. The shoulder-length hair of his head and short beard was gray-blond, the gray beginning to take control. Other than that he was hairless except for the blond thatching in his pits and a luxurious blond bush, in which nestled the prize cock and balls of the regiment—his championship equipment contributing to why he was the captain of the guard. Many of the other guardsmen had indulged in body tattooing. Mahir only had a double row of black notches running down either side of his trunk, ominously celebrating the men he had dispatched in battle.

Mahir kissed Asu on the neck and in the hollow of his shoulders, and on his ears, taking those into his mouth and licking around them, before putting his lips next to Asu's ear and speaking softly, in a deep voice.

"You cannot escape your destiny, young man. But you can control it and learn to use it and let yourself revel in it. You have a beauty that makes men dribble, a small size that makes men feel more the man, and a very nice set of privates . . ." Here Mahir stopped cupping Asu's cock and balls and moved the hand back to where it parted Asu's buttocks cheeks and found and gently rubbed Asu's entrance, already conditioned to pucker and open to the touch. ". . . the plumpest orbs I've parted in some time—I can hardly wait to part them with more than my fingers—and a hole that, though now a bit swollen, is fit for a king's cock. Perhaps after a few months in the wine shops . . ."

"You are so different. You make it sound so different," Asu murmured. "Not like the soldiers out there, not like the men in the wine shop. You speak to me, saying things that make me stir. But in the end you are going to take me too, aren't you."

"Oh yes, little one. In the end I am going to cock you too. I'm going to cock you as you have not yet been plowed. I did not bring you in here just for a fatherly chat. But, although well meaning—and for your own good—Nasri and the men

159

were using the wrong approach with you, I think. As he tells it, it was not unwillingness or rejection of your destiny that made you resistant, but it was fear of the cock, a hating of it possessing you. Is that not so?"

Asu did not answer, but Mahir could feel him already relaxing in his grip. His free hand was roaming all over Asu's body, gliding over the curves, into the crevices, covering the young man's breasts and rubbing the now-engorged nipples.

"When we are done here, you will love the cock. You will see it as your gate to riches and pleasure. You will understand your body as the key to open the hearts and purses of other men, within days or weeks—which must be finished before I can bring you back into the palace—you will be totally conditioned to the largest of men. You already have had the largest of men to be had in the kingdom. From tonight, it will be you controlling men, with your beauty, for as long as it lasts. And if you're clever enough, when the beauty has given out, the riches will sustain you. And when you are properly conditioned, no longer sore down here from the preparations of the palace guardsmen, you will have only pleasure—your own pleasure—from the cocks."

"I can obtain pleasure—my own pleasure—from the . . . the cock?" Asu murmured. He was panting in shallow breaths at the attentions of Mahir's hand on his body. And his voice was slightly slurred, thick with something he had not yet identified as arousal.

He did, however, realize that his own cock was engorging at the touch of Mahir's hand and fingers. Mahir began a slow, sensuous stroking of Asu's cock.

"Yes, before you leave my bed, you will be begging for the cock. And you will have pleasure. You have pleasure now, do you not? Did any of my soldiers bother to do this for you?"

Asu shook his head in a negative. He could not speak through his low moans and groans. This indeed was pleasure, this stroking of his cock. All of his attention was now riveted to the hand stroking his cock.

"There are pleasures to be had in the act, little one. Pleasures that you can demand and control, while still demanding rich rewards. And soon, very soon, riding the cock will be second nature to you. You can then concentrate on getting your enjoyment as much from having it inside you as you do from the rewards it brings in."

"I don't know. I can't imagine . . . I'm so frightened."

"Think beyond the wine shop. Think of being in the palace and of riding the cock of a king. He is expert, but he is not built like his palace guardsmen are. He will give you pleasures you can only imagine now, without taxing your guts as the soldiers did . . . or as I am about to do."

Asu squirmed a bit within Mahir's embrace.

"Yes, little one, as I am about to do. The guardsmen who snatched your virginity, your first soldier, Nasri, is in training to succeed me—someday. He is being trained in the positions of India. He thought that what you needed was a rough taking to prepare you for the wine shop. After seeing you—and yes I have heard about your charms from the talk of the street—I believe you should be conditioned to the king's bed. While you are in the wine shop, I will send Nasri to you, and he will teach you the positions of India. But tonight, little one. Tonight you are mine—your sweet hole is a sheath for my thick sword. I wish to be inside you when you are still tight, before you are slack. Your walls will be stretched to the point of split. You have yet to be cocked as I am going to cock you."

Asu groaned and nearly fainted, with Mahir still holding him close.

This was part of the conditioning. Mahir was pushing Asu to the brink with the imagery of what was to come. This was all part of the foreplay that his guardsmen had not learned helped in the battle.

Asu moaned, close to ejaculation, his hips in motion, with Mahir having loosened the grip on the cock to permit Asu to stroke inside his encircling beefy fingers. Mahir placed his index finger on Asu's piss slit and pressed into it while his teeth went to Asu's ear and gently pressed into and scraped along the lobe. With a cry—which he still did not know was ecstasy—Asu breathily announced that he was about to explode inside.

Quick as can be, Mahir released both Asu's cock and his body and had turned both himself and Asu so that Mahir was kneeling in front of Asu, supporting Asu's body in a half crouch,

161

with a strong arm around the small of his back. Asu's torso was arched back, away from Mahir. Mahir's mouth covered Asu's cock, and his free hand went to Asu's ball sac. He gently pulled Asu's balls down from his body and then squeezed the balls, again gently. With a howl of release, Asu ejaculated down the Palace Guard captain's throat.

"Tell me now that you cannot get pleasure from your destiny," Mahir said as he lifted Asu and lowered the young man's shuddering body, belly down, on the sleeping couch.

Asu felt his legs being moved apart and the knees of the captain come down between them. He sensed the massive torso hovering over his back. He felt the warm breath on the back of his neck and then the kiss there. He turned his head and saw the heavily muscled arm, with its puckered battle scars, planted firmly on a gigantic closed fist at the side of his shoulder. He felt the bulb of the cock—the monster cock—at his hole. It was being rubbed across his entrance. And then taken away and slapped against his buttocks cheeks. Then back to the hole, rubbing across it, stopping to pulsate at his entrance, pressing in, but just a bit, back to rubbing, sliding along his perineum to the base of his ball sac, and then back to rubbing across his entrance. He only barely realized that he was raising his pelvis to the cock, widening his stance, anticipating the invasion, as he had done for the guardsmen when he knew they were going to slide into him—almost revealing, to anyone but himself, that he wanted it.

"Such a small body," Mahir was whispering in his ear. "A small, tight channel, even after the attentions of my soldiers. But mine the largest cock of all, none that you have had, none that you will have will fill you as this one will. Sliding slowly inside you, into your stomach, your walls stretching to the limit— almost beyond the limit—no matter what angle you give it, how far apart you spread your legs and your plump buttocks. And then the start of me moving in and out, in and out, inside you . . ."

Asu moaned deeply. "Master . . . please."
"Please what, little one?"
"Please."

Mahir laughed, and then Asu sensed the captain withdrawing from him, moving down on the couch. Strong hands, on each side, lifted Asu's pelvis with hand holds underneath him, gripping him and raising him between his groin and the tops of his thighs. The sense of warm breath on his swollen hole. The cool touch of a tongue, starting tentatively but gaining in command and demand.

The long sigh. Asu not realizing that it came from him. He had moaned again too, but now he sensed something more. He was sighing. And visions of that cock flooded his mind. Sliding into him, filling him, moving inside him.

"Please," he weakly murmured, moving his pelvis in almost imperceptible motion back and forth against the tongue.

The pressure of a finger. Moving inside, revolving, finding his prostrate—a feeling of need and of urgency that Asu had never felt before. Both a pleasure and a want that he'd never imagined feeling. A hand encasing his cock, stroking it. Not gently now—fast, hard pulls. Milking him.

"Please!" Asu screamed to the stone ceiling as he exploded again and then collapsed, into an exhausted half sleep.

The dream was sensual, full of pleasure. The man covering him handsome and regal, a crown of golden leaves encircling his brow. His purple silken thawb pulled up to his waist, a golden chain and a swinging medallion around his neck as his torso hovered above Asu. Asu could see one of his own legs running up the man's torso, the other one being held up and out by a well-manicured hand, heavy with jeweled rings. The man was stroking inside him, but Asu's pelvis was just as active, counterthrusting, trying to pull the cock in as far as those of the soldiers Asu had known and of the powerful Zeus of a guard captain. Asu's hands were on the man's chest underneath his thawb, working the coin-sized, hard nipples. Working the man, working for the pleasure and rewards of the man, but working for Asu's own pleasure too.

Asu woke, stretched out on his side on the animal skins-covered couch. The captain was stretched behind him, embracing him and gliding his hands on Asu's body. Asu's topmost thigh was raised and resting on the closed legs of the beefy soldier chief. The bulb of Mahir's cock was resting against Asu's entrance.

"Ah, awake are we, little bird? Pleasant dreams?"

"Umm," Asu answered, only half awake, but aware that he was moving from imagined pleasure to real pleasure. He turned his face to Mahir's, who, for the first time in the night, moved his lips to Asu's, pressed them open with his tongue, and fully possessed Asu's mouth. Asu groaned for him. Mahir moved a hand to his hard cock and revolved the bulb around the rim of Asu's hole. Asu groaned more deeply. Mahir raised the knee of his upper leg and placed his foot flat on the surface of the couch. This raised Asu's leg and turned his pelvis more toward Mahir's groin. Asu could feel his hole open more—blossoming, throbbing, ready and wanting now for the slide of the cock. So could Mahir. The bulb moved inside, just the bulb, though. Mahir revolved the bulb inside the hole entrance. Then, to the tune of deeper moans from Asu and the heaving of Asu's belly and the sound of his pants, Mahir pressed the bulb in a bit, then pulled it out. In and out, in and out—still just at the surface. Revolve. The entrance was open, sucking at the bulb.

Asu pulled away from the kiss. "Please!"

"Please what?"

"Please. I beg you. Give me the cock! Put me to the sword."

"Ah, you beg me now for it, do you? I told you you would, didn't I? You are realizing that the act can be as much for your pleasure as for the other man's now, aren't you? That you can make that happen, control it. I assure you that you have me; that I am desperate to be inside you. The only reason I could hold back is that I knew I was going to cock you, whether or not you asked for it. But I am as much yours at this moment as you are mine. You can seize your destiny rather than shrink from it."

"Oh, the gods, oh, the gods. Put me to the cock now. I beg you."

"You may have it now, yes. But to complete your conditioning—and so that you know it is done—you may only have the cock one way. You will ride it yourself."

Mahir lay on his back, his fists locked behind his head, looking—at least initially, amused and triumphant—as, facing

164

him, Asu straddled his midsection with his knees, his channel—through no little effort—sunk on Mahir's cock, and rode him in languid motion.

"I . . . I . . . didn't know," Asu murmured in a thick, dreamy voice.

Asu's body was too beautiful and desirable for Mahir to yield control for long, though, and Mahir had held off longer than he would want—certainly longer than he thought he could, although, with this young beauty he did, indeed, have a prize for a king, a toy he could gift the king in exchange for the king's continued good favor. This was a primary function of the captain of the king's guard. To condition and provide young, pliable, beautiful male bodies for the king's bed.

Asu was riding his cock well, leaning back, grabbing his ankles, and rising and falling on the cock by leveraging with his knees and calves. His eyes had a glassy, cum-filled look in them—and, indeed, the ride was cushioned by the cum of several guardsmen—and he was babbling almost incoherently, permitting himself to be lost in the pleasure of the cock now. Mahir had not a shred of doubt that the youth was fully conditioned, fully enjoying what he was getting.

But the scene, the experience, was much too arousing for Mahir too. He could take no more. With a roar, he raised his torso, grabbed Asu by the waist, and called out in a commanding voice, "Give over the cocking to me now. You have done well. Just lay back and enjoy it."

Dutifully, Asu let his torso relax in a backward arc, his arms dangling at his side, as Mahir began pulling Asu's channel up and down on his cock, slowly at first, but increasingly faster, deeper, harder.

"Yes, cock me! Put me to the cock me! Cock me!" Asu cried to the stone ceiling.

Harder and harder, faster and faster. Brutally slamming the huge cock inside the small, but accommodating body. Breathing heavily, chanting a war chant, losing all control over this beautiful, young body. Rising to new heights of arousal himself because the little one was dancing the cock now. Crying out for it, writhing and throwing his little body around. The little body taking it hard and deep, sucking it deep inside. Climbing to

165

the heights of the cock, slamming himself down to the depths of it. Spouting out on Mahir's belly, causing the flood to work its way up from inside Mahir's balls. This would be a big blow, even for Mahir. He could feel it boiling, rising up from inside him.

* * * *

Asu didn't make it back to the wine shop until the next afternoon. Mahir could not let him go until both were beyond exhaustion. And Asu sobbed that he didn't want to go, and was only assuaged when Mahir whispered an assurance in his ear that, when it came to bed partners, what was the king's was also Mahir's.

Hatim, after being assured that Asu was fully ready to accept his fate and his position in life now, assigned Asu to a room in the back of the shop and let him sleep and heal for three days.

On the night of the third day, however, a naked Asu was sitting on the cock of an obviously happy and aroused Sargon in the same chair that Asu had wriggled away from him in four nights previously. Without command to do so, Asu was leveraging on the balls of his feet on the floor on either side of Sargon's lap and was rising and falling on the cock, such as it was—requiring no effort for Asu after the soldier cocks he had recently known. It was all that Sargon could imagine wanting, though. Asu was saying all of the things that Sargon wanted to hear about how wonderful Asu's sponsor was to him. Sargon was strumming the beautiful young man's nipples and savoring the victory of his long campaign, having no idea how short the time of his sponsoring and recompense would be. Sargon was alternating the stroke of his hands between Asu's cock and his nipples—because Asu demanded the attention of him and Sargon was too much the slave of Asu's channel now not to give the young beauty what he demanded.

Asu's performance was helped by two factors. He was so soused with free wine provided by Hatim that he didn't particularly care who was fucking him, as long as there was a pile of cash on the table in front of him—and as he rose and fell on Sargon's cock, he was looking over to where the soldier Nasri

166

was standing at the end of the bar table and looking at him. Later, after the wine shop closed, Nasri would be taking Asu to Asu's little room behind the wine shop and would resume teaching him new sexual positions of India that were sure to increase what men were willing to pay for Asu's body. And in just weeks, the palace, the king—and Mahir. And Nasri had said that the king knew the positions of India better than he did, was more flexible than he, and would give Asu even more pleasure, despite the differences in the cocks, while taking his own, than even Nasri could give him. It was doubtful Nasri actually believed that, but he was as much the king's man as Captain Mahir was.

The basic training of Asu had been concluded satisfactorily for all.

So You Want to Be in Movies

"So, my agent said it was for some sort of commercials for the Halloween season."

"Yes, that's right. It's for commercial use to be released a few weeks before Halloween, yes."

I needed the work. The plays on Broadway were shutting down almost as fast as they opened. It was just bad luck, a bunch of new plays that weren't piquing the audiences' interest and some tired old revivals. There was more creative work being done off Broadway and in some clubs. I liked doing those, but they didn't pay too well. I was barely getting by.

"I've looked at a bunch of résumés that were sent to me by the New York agents, and yours was one of the standouts. Good enough for us to pay your way down here."

"Yes, I was surprised to get a call from here. New York isn't exactly—"

"New York has a freer environment overall. It's where our best talent comes from."

I didn't want to argue myself out of a possible gig, so I didn't pursue that point. The pay would be good. Real, real good for the number of hours it should entail. And commercials. They were great exposure for guys trying to break into movies. Which was what I was trying to do. Me and thousands of other young, good-looking guys, I'd found. But I had talent. I'd been in two Broadway plays, one with a small speaking part. If either one had lasted more than two weeks, I would have been sitting pretty. And I was doing OK in Off Broadway and in the private clubs. Of course, the sooner I could get out of the private clubs, the better.

We were sitting in the out-door section of a café above the Virginia Beach boardwalk, and I was dividing my time between listening to the Holland guy and watching a volleyball game going on between muscle studs in their tiny Speedos below us. These obviously were guys more there to be seen than to play volleyball.

Andrew Holland was quite a looker too. He was the film producer who had paid my way down here. I was looking past him at the table down at the volleyball players and there wasn't much difference between him and them other than age—and I wasn't at all sure I didn't give him the edge on desirability.

He was the mature Paul Newman type—with watery blue eyes, good facials, and silver gray hair, which, on him, as was the case occasionally, made him look younger than a guy should be with a full head of gray hair. He had a nice smile, and I liked that he was keeping this interview balanced—selling me on his project as much as testing me for suitability for the gig. He had a smooth and easy delivery. A perfect salesman type, but one of million-dollar projects, not used Edsels. He also, from what I could see, was as cut—especially for his age—as any of the young guys at the volleyball net. He was wearing a silver-gray-colored sports coat, but under that was a form-fitting black polo shirt. It all went perfectly well with the watery blue eyes, open smile, and perfectly cut gray hair.

The only incongruity I noticed, and I had no idea how to even ask about it, was that he was wearing close-fitting black-leather gloves. It didn't seem to limit the dexterity of his hands, though. There had been no hesitation or awkwardness in picking up his beer glass. He seemed completely at home in the gloves. But I kept looking at those gloves as he talked.

I had no idea how I had gotten there. I was bound, naked, in a spread X, on my back, on a bondage table, my mouth gagged with a ball gag. A man in a devil's mask and black cape, but otherwise naked except for black-leather gloves and a studded chest harness, was standing next to the table, hovering over me, slowly stroking my cock. His build was mature and I could see the gray hair above the devil's mask, but his body was trim and well-muscled. He was hard, and what he was swinging was nothing to laugh at. I was already hard too and was raising my pelvis to the jacking, curling my trapped fingers and toes, and pulling hard at the bonds. Wanting to be free, but not for escape anymore. No, I wanted to do more in the sexual encounter. His stroking, going off beat now and then to make me shudder, was driving me crazy. Relentlessly stroking me, sending me high above the clouds. I came, but he didn't stop stroking. He slowed down from the crescendo he'd reached, but he didn't stop. It was painful at first, and I begged in muffled sounds through the gag for relief, but he didn't stop, bringing me hard again and then to another ejaculation. Pulling on my cock with that gloved hand. No sense of the passage of time, knowing only that he had been at it for a long time. Starting for a third time . . .

He was mounting the bondage table, straddling my chest. He freed me of the ball gag, cupped my head in his hands, and presented his hard cock for sucking. The pubic hair nesting his cock was black with streaks of gray. Curly; smelt of musk. My chance to participate more in the sexual encounter.

". . . specialty films, really."

My attention came back to the present. Holland was leaning over the table, deeper into a sales pitch. It wasn't a pitch he needed to give me. He had me at the fee quote—and the anticipation that it would be shown on TV. Commercials. Advertising I didn't have to pay for, one way or the other. And in New York, payment in the entertainment world didn't always come in the form of cash. If he wanted me to get up from this table and go with him to nail down the audition, I was prepared to go. I can't say I didn't want to go.

In the New York world, he'd said.

"Why Virginia Beach, down in Virginia?" I asked, not even aware of why I asked, but needing to get back into the conversation, needing not to reveal that I had been off into a disturbing fantasy. I was trying to keep my eyes off the tight-fitting black gloves. I thought that it would make him mad for me to draw attention them. But he was expressive when he talked. They were waving in front of my face. There was no way I could avoid looking at them.

"The Navy mostly—and production costs. Lots of naval presence here, and it's actually cheaper to bring whoever we need down from New York or out from Los Angeles than to pay the New York or California production prices."

Los Angeles. I ached to be in Los Angeles. In movies.

"The Navy? You do training films?"

"Yes, we do a lot of training films. Navy guys are naturals for that. That's sort of what this film is about too. Demonstrating how the technique we're showing is done."

My attention was arrested by the volleyball game down on the beach. It had been disbanded. There were still two studly looking guys down there, though. One was backed up against a light pole at the edge of the sand, his arms drawn above his head and his fists clutching the stem of the pole above him. The other guy was leaning close in to him with a hand on his waist, speaking low and seemingly intensely to the other guy. I was projecting the kiss—and was both titillated and surprised at the image occurring right out here on the open public beach. But they just stood there for a while and then both turned and walked off. They walked close together, though, the one guy's arm around the waist of the other guy, holding him in close to the hip and giving the impression of having full control. Climbing the steps, walking to the entrance to the ocean-side lobby of the hotel next to where we were sitting. The two guys turned their eyes to each other. The face I could see was of the guy being led. There were mixed signals there, I thought. He turned back toward the ocean front at the door, almost as if he was going to pull back, walk away. There were two hands on his waist now, though, turning him back to the Hotel entrance, gently pushing him inside.

I was bound wrists and ankles, standing facing and bound to a Saint Andrew's cross inside a room painted all in black. I was looking at a full-length mirror mounted on the wall across the room, so I could watch it all. I could see a mound of black material through the bottom of the legs of the cross that my legs were spread and bound to. The material spilled out around the edges of the cross limbs. It was moving, undulating, in a rhythm that I could feel all the way through my naked body. My cock had been pulled between my legs and was being sucked by an expert mouth—a mouth and throat that could take me deep and hold me inside, throbbing. Keep me gasping for breath. A hand laced my balls between its leather-covered fingers, pulling them out from my body and squeezing and rolling them. I got the full effect of my facial expressions through the V of the top of the cross—my mouth open and slack, my eyes slitted in combined pain and ecstasy. Breathing heavy, panting. I could clearly hear my own moans. My cock was free except that the hand worrying my balls had moved a gloved finger to encase the root of the staff. My entrance was being rimmed and flicked with a tongue. The tongue was pressing inside. The finger encircling the base of my cock tightened its squeeze. My balls were being rolled and pulled.

I could hear a voice murmuring weakly, "Fuck me. Please fuck me now." I only belatedly realized that it was my own voice.

And the answering laugh. I could not get the raspy answering laugh out of my mind.

When I had come, the figure rose behind me, and the mask of a devil face, topped with silver-gray hair, appeared over my shoulder. A black-gloved hand cupped my chin and pulled my head back, as I felt another gloved hand cupping my buttocks and then helping to guide the cap of a hard cock at the rim of my hole. A long cock slid and slid and slid up into me. I felt the sliver studs of the chest harness rubbing on my back. I cried out my welcome— "Yes, yes, YES!"—and began moving my hips against the building plowing of the cock inside me, pulling at my bindings, wanting some form of control and way to signal that I didn't need to be held captive to want this. A freeing that no form of begging was granting me.

"Excuse me. Exactly what sort of commercials are these?" I asked as I once more became aware of the film producer sitting across from me, leaning into me, smiling his mature Paul Newman smile, and, now, with a gloved hand on my thigh under the table, squeezing my thigh gently—in a rhythm that was reminiscent of the rhythm of the stroking in my St. Andrew's cross fantasy.

"Not commercials, exactly. Commercial films. Ones that make very good money and that could give you exposure for larger roles in larger films."

"I'm not sure I—"

I was getting the drift of this. Exposure. Exposure indeed. But I couldn't form words to respond before he broke in, pressing the sell. I didn't even know what I wanted to say. The feel of that gloved hand on my thigh was robbing my brain of thought.

"It was Jake Plaugher who put us on to your agent. Jake Plaugher is a friend of ours. He's made some films with his. I believe he is a special friend of yours too. Is that not so?"

Jake Plaugher. I tensed. He was saying that he knew what I let Jake Plaugher do to me. It wasn't just that this man wanted me to go with him to audition on my back for a film gig.

His voice was low, almost singsong in texture, drawing me in. "In and out, in and out—the slide of the cock—coupled with the helpless pull at the bindings. That's such a visual image, isn't it? Just like these gloves are. You haven't asked about the gloves. I wear them to provide a visual image of what might be, what is to come, what can be yours if you give yourself to me. And I'm a visual man." Holland's mature Paul Newman smile was mesmerizing, but something in the smile was changing. "And the image of giving over all control to another . . . to a real expert in the sensual . . . a man who can give you what you need . . ."

He didn't finish that sentence. I had interjected a strangled moan, surfaced not only from the images he had spun but also from the black-gloved hand he had moved to my basket. I only then was aware that I had slid down on my chair, my tailbone at the front edge, to permit the hand, which had been slowly working its way up my thigh, to reach my crotch. I had raised one of my feet to his chair, resting it beside his rump, and he was gripping my ankle in his other gloved hand, holding it there, tightly, in thrall, for a brief moment. No matter how brief the moment, though, I felt the sense of the imprisonment, of the control he was asserting.

"Come," Holland said, rising, and putting out his gloved hand. "The studio isn't far from here. We can have you back on a plane to New York this evening. We've arranged for Jake Plaugher to meet you at JFK upon your return and to put you up for the night. I understand Jake has unusual ways to put you up. We can be just as inventive as Jake is, though—in fact, you might decide you are too exhausted to accept Jake's offer. But it will be an exhaustion that leaves you humming. And, who knows, maybe you won't want to return to New York at all."

Hearing his raspy laugh—a shudderingly familiar laugh—at his own joke, I looked up into his face. Was this the face of the man I had sat down at the table with?

"Come be a part of our Halloween special. Come. I can fulfill your darkest fantasies—and immortalize them on film. You do have dark fantasies, don't you?"

He knew. I could almost believe now that he had invoked them.

Seeing him now, the expression on his face, the change that had come into it, I wondered. The man in my fantasies. Was he wearing a mask at all in those fantasies—or was this the face of that man?

Trembling, I rose, and put my hand—and the next several hours of my time and freedom; only that, if I was lucky—in his black-leather gloved hand as he turned me with the other hand on my waist and guided me out of the café and into the backseat of a chauffeured black limousine.

175

Mentoring

Is this the very café table where we sat? Yes, I think it is. In fact, I'm sure it is. It's as if time has stood still. The café is just as it was nearly thirty years ago—or at least I don't remember anything as different. It's hard to believe that as much as London has changed over the last twenty years, Norwich might not have changed at all. Or so it seems. And so I want it to be. I don't want to have been wrong; I don't want Norwich to have outdistanced me. I left Norwich for London precisely because nothing had been changing in my life. I was in a rut; one of poverty and of unfulfilling dreams. I made sacrifices and compromises—tremendous ones—to change my life.

Do I regret it? Is the possibility of that why I've avoided returning here?

I don't have an opportunity to pursue that train of thought, as the waiter is at my elbow asking if everything is to my satisfaction.

"Yes, thank you. Yes, I'll take another coffee, thank you."

I don't know whether the waiter had recognized me or if it was the cut and material of my suit or the manicured appearance of the body I work hard and spend mightily to keep trim. Or whether it is the patrician demeanor I acquired during the decades in London that is according me such close attention from the wait staff, but it is clear that I am getting more attention than anyone else in the café. It's true that I'm recognized occasionally on the streets of London now— especially after my most recent series of exhibitions and the media coverage of that—but I'd hardly be remembered in Norwich, I shouldn't think.

But, of course they may receive the same magazines here that are sold on the streets of London.

Twenty-six years. It has been that long since I've been in Norwich. I was a struggling art student at the time, bypassing university not only because my family couldn't afford it, but also because I was just busting with the need to create—and determined not to work in the textile factory my whole life. I would have done anything at the time to be given the time and support needed to get on with the painting.

I, in fact, did what was required to get that done.

* * * *

Martin Ashen had been all the rage in Norwich. He had been to London and even to the continent with his art exhibits—not just his painting of seascapes and ships but also with his bronze sculptures. And now he was back in Norwich, mentoring at the Norfolk Art Institute.

He wasn't lecturing or teaching. When he wasn't rendering works of art for his series of life in the textile mills of the city, he was roaming the studios of the institute, giving advice to the students, and picking one or two out for, as he called it, mentoring. Producing art on such a mundane subject as the working-class textile workers in nineteenth century mills was just catching on in England. Surely Master Ashen was at the forefront of this movement, I thought—although I was later to learn that he actually was late to that medium and had come to Norwich to catch up with some of his contemporaries who were riding a social awareness wave and had already overworked more industrial subjects in the country.

178

"The line is good, but the perspective is off," the rich, melodic voice cut into my concentration from over my shoulder. "Here, I think it can be readily fixed."

I trembled as Master Ashen took the brush out of my hand and, leaning into me close, applied four deft strokes to the canvas I was working on. I could readily see how, with just that, he'd brought the painting under a control I had known was absent but had no idea how to fix.

I was mortified, and that must not have been hidden from him. Putting the brush down in the trough of the easel rather than handing it back to me, he put his hand on my shoulder and squeezed gently.

"All in good time," he said. "I can see the talent is there. It just needs more practice—and perhaps a little closer observation of the work of others."

"I'm . . . sorry," I stammered. "I don't think I can—"

"Never say 'I can't,' young man"—he almost thundered that, causing nearby artists to look around, either startled or with self-satisfied looks that I was being upbraided. This, to my consternation, included Howard, an artist a few years my senior who had taken an interest in my work—and in whom, I must admit, I was taking a more personal interest. "I said the talent was there," Ashen continued—and I think his thought that I was discounting that was more the source of his flash of anger than what I had said—"it is patience and a bit more attention to detail you now need to apply."

He moved on right after that, but my frustration and disappointment in myself lingered. I couldn't concentrate on the landscape I was working on further that afternoon, so I put my tools away and left early. I took my sketch pad with me, though, and walked swiftly to Chapelfield Gardens, a recently opened park near the city center, which was the setting of the painting I was working on. The master painter had criticized my observation skills, so I wanted to take in the perspective of my subject matter again. I wanted to see better what I may have missed in my earlier trips.

My sighting was from just inside the tree line of a stand of trees overlooking a small, circular Roman temple on a hillock with a pond and a line of trees beyond it.

That wasn't the only reason I went to the park, though. I wanted to know if Howard would follow me here. We had met here earlier when we both were sketching the scene. I believed my sketches were better than Howard's, but of course I would not tell him that. He had been working at the art college three years longer than I had.

But it wasn't only sketching we'd done here. He read me poetry too and we discussed our lives and our ambitions. And we increasingly were becoming more intimate with each visit here. I had given little thought to relations between one man and another—but Howard was opening my eyes to so many possibilities I had not given thought to before. We had not reached the stage of ultimate intimacy—or what Howard had described as a luxury of life that would bring pleasure beyond measure—although I had tasted his lips and seen the glimmer of an opening to the pleasures he spoke of. And his hands had awakened me even more to the opportunities we seemed to be moving to—when and as I overcame my inhibitions to the unknown and the fear of what Howard's world entailed.

I settled under a tree and turned an intense gaze on the Roman temple. Surprisingly details came to me that I hadn't noticed before. Eager at this unexpected confirmation of what Martin Ashen had told me I needed to do, I plucked a pencil from the box I had brought, turned the sketch pad to a new page, and instead of looking at and trying to sketch the whole sweep of the view before me, I concentrated on separate sketches of just a detail here and a detail there of what I was seeing anew.

So intent was I on sketching that I didn't hear Howard approach until he was nearly upon me, and when he spoke to me, it caused my pencil to slide across the page and ruin my drawing of the detail of the cornice work on one of the temple columns.

But I didn't care. Howard was here.

"He can't believe your age."

"Who can't believe my age?" I asked him, looking up and feeling the usual catch in my breath when I saw his well-muscled body in the dappled sunlight filtering through the leaves of the trees overhead.

"The master from London—Martin Ashen. He was sure that you were too young to be enrolled in the institute."

"He asked my age? He wants me to be dismissed?"

"Quite the opposite if I read him right," Howard answered as he flopped down beside me and put an arm around my shoulders. His other hand went to my thigh as I sat cross-legged under the tree. "I do believe he fancies you. And I noted a bit of disappointment in his voice when I told him you were in your majority."

"I guess that's why he said he thought I had talent," I said. "He thought I was younger and therefore not having had time to develop any skill."

"You always belittle yourself, Philip," Howard said. "And when you do that, you fail to see where your opportunities lie. You do not see the main chance."

"Like I do not yet see my subject matter in detail yet?" I asked. ". . . as the master artist told me?"

"Something like that. You are indeed young, Philip. And not just in visage."

I was breathing hard and leaning into him. The hand on my thigh was roaming. It felt hot to the touch. I wanted him to take the next step with me; I could not be the one to take it. But he seemed to be holding back. Before he had moved as boldly as he thought he dared at each of our meetings out here on the verge of the trees. Now I was clinging closely to him in his embrace, relaxed, ready for him, my lips open, my willingness obvious in other ways.

But he was pulling away from me and standing. I could tell from his breathing that this was hard for him to do.

"I am quite sure he is impressed with your talent, Philip. In fact, he has sent me out here to tell you that he wishes you to meet with him in the café by the Wensum River. Now, as a matter of fact."

"And that is pleasing enough to you?" I asked, in disbelief. Why was Howard running cold with me now. He was hinting that the master wanted to meet with me for something more than discussing my painting—or his. Why did this not displease Howard? Even if it was about the art, why was Howard deferring his need and desire to mine?

"Pleasing enough under the circumstances, yes," Howard said, only half turned to me and looking away. "There will be time for us."

Heavy of heart when I knew I should be euphoric, I had risen from the ground, and I walked away from him, without saying another word or looking back.

* * * *

"Model for a painting and a sculpture?" I asked, confused and surprised. I thought we were meeting at the café—at least ostensibly—to talk about Master Ashen helping me with my painting technique.

"I wish to mentor your work, of course," Ashen said hurriedly, placing a hand on my arm. "But you are unusually young looking. I've been looking for the perfect face and form to represent the draw boy in my textile factory series. Come to my studio and sit for me for those works—and, certainly, I will mentor your painting. I will even take you to London with me so you can continue your studies in more advantageous circumstances."

"You would take me to London too?" I asked. "And mentor my studies. And all I have to do is sit for you to represent a draw boy at the loom in a textile factory?" I knew what a draw boy did. Like many of the local men, I had worked in the textile factories when I was a boy. And I had done it longer than most, because I was smaller than most. The job of perching above the loom and carrying the weft thread through in advance of the flying shuttle and thereby creating the pattern of different-colored threads in the cloth went to those with small, dexterous hands.

"I believe that you understand that there would be more required of you," Master Ashen said.

And I certainly did understand. The palm of his hand had centered between my thighs under the café table. He was making quite clear what he expected in return for his offer.

"I will pay you the regular fee, of course, for sitting for me. And I will take you to London with me and you will become a great artist—because of the mentoring I give you. But you

182

must lie under me as well, willingly. I don't want you to misunderstand what the contract is."

What was that Howard had said—that I was not mature enough to take my opportunities when they came to me? I did want to go to London. I did want to become a great artist. As for the other, I felt I was ready for that too—although I thought it would be with Howard.

I sat for Master Ashen twice for the casting of the bronze statue and three times for the painting. I was posed by a loom, stripped to the waist, to show the heat and strenuous requirements of factory atmosphere, and with my fingers pushing threads into place below a descending shuttle, my close concentration on what I was doing a focus of the art work. He arranged the lighting so that a beam of light fell on my face and chest while, other than that, the scene was in shadows. The painting was rendered in sepia colors.

He concluded each of the "draw boy" sessions by coming between me and the loom, pulling my trousers off my legs, parting my thighs, hunching over me with just his hard cock exposed through the fly in his own trousers, and fucking me to his ejaculation.

"The Draw Boy" is what he titled both of the factory works, and you can visit the painting at London's Harrow Museum of art even today. Ashen kept the sculpture in his own collection after exhibiting it, and it has disappeared into a private collection.

After sex he would take up his sketch pad and do post-coital pencil sketches of me. When he ultimately was forced to depart London—and England altogether—under charges of pedophilia some ten years later, he caused quite a sensation in France by exhibiting these sketches—in a large collection of more young men he "mentored" than just me. By the end of the exhibit all of the sketches had been bought and disappeared into private collections.

On the eve of my own exhibition at the National Gallery in London some years later, I received one of these sketches of me after sex in the post. There was no indication it had been sent by Martin, but I knew it had been. It was his way of reminding me how I had gotten to where I was in the art world.

I knew that it wasn't an expression of any desire to have me again because, by then, it was well established that it was only younger-looking lads he was interested in.

I had known that lying under him was part of the arrangement. But still, the first time he fucked me, I was surprised and taken aback. There was little preparation or warning. He just said that I could relax from my pose and came walking at me, his shirt unbuttoned to the waist and his hard cock, held in his hand, thrusting out of his trousers. He was a big man, giving the impression that he was heavier than average. I was to learn, though, that most of that was muscle and that it gave him the strength to do whatever he wanted with me.

I would have wished that the first time would be a little more tender and meaningful and less matter of fact than that. And I would have wished it from Howard.

Martin had the hands of an artist, long, slender, yet strong fingers. His cock was of greater than average size and that it curved up so that while he was fucking me from above, he would move with a pronounced dip and upward thrust. His complexion was florid; his hair the red of an Irishman, and his chest and arms pelted with curly hair.

He was not a handsome man, and while he was fucking me, he showed a visage of cruelty and anger, although after that first time, when I was in considerable pain and begged him to stop or at least to work me more slowly but he completely ignored me in deference to his own need and desire, I came to understand that he was just intense and focused in the act rather than angry.

He sometimes couldn't resist fucking me again after doing his post-coital sketch and when he did so, he took me more slowly and I received more enjoyment from the cocking.

After the second modeling session, Howard asked me to meet him in the park at our usual place and there, with little preliminary steps and with the assurance that I would lay under him too, Howard gently pushed me down on my back, first undressed me and then himself, pushed his knees under my buttocks, and gave me the long, slow, deep fucking that I had dreamed of.

After we had both come, I sobbed silently into his shoulder as he held me close, and still buried inside me, rocked me back and forth in his embrace.

"I didn't hurt you, did I?" he asked, the concern in his voice evident.

"No. This was how I dreamed it would be," I murmured. "Why didn't you give me this before I went to Martin Ashen? This was what I wanted the first time."

"I'm sorry, but it was part of the arrangement."

"The arrangement?"

"He wanted to be the first with you. He said he would take me to London too if he was first. I didn't think it would matter to you. It doesn't, does it, after all?"

"No, of course not," I whispered into his shoulder. But of course it did matter to me. It mattered very much. It just wasn't something that could be changed.

Ashen did take us both to London, just as he promised. And he did mentor my talent and skills into my becoming a renowned artist. His taking of me continued for a brief time in London—and I let him do whatever he wanted with me in exchange for the opportunities he was giving me in the art world. His interest was only brief, though, as I grew and matured. I no longer looked young to him, and his interests turned to ever-younger men—and then boys, before he was cornered and exposed for his proclivities and was forced to go abroad.

Howard was only with us for a month in London. As I feared, his talent was not up to the larger art community. And, having already gotten what he wanted from Howard, Ashen's interest in mentoring him was never complete.

I let Howard go more easily than he thought I would. His loving was good up to the end, but I never could be completely comfortable with the choice he had made for me.

* * * *

Ah, the memories of twenty-six years ago. I haven't been back to Norwich since—until now. I was afraid of what I might find—that I would learn that my life here as a child and a youth

185

was one of squalor that I barely escaped, even though the cost was high. Or worse, I have been afraid that I'd find that there was something noble here and clean that I sold cheaply.

What I found, though, was that it was difficult for me to remember the city at all—or much of my life or of what I did here or dreamt here. Sometimes I try to think of Howard as the first love of my life. But I find I can't picture him at all. And I have no idea what happened to him. A big fear of mine is that perhaps he returned here and is working at the Norfolk Art Institute. And that he will think I should remember him or, heaven forbid, that I should fall under his spell again.

I wouldn't be here at all if it wouldn't be remarked that I had left Norfolk—the shire of my own upbringing—out in this portfolio of art I'm putting together for the National Museum on the regional characteristics of people in Great Britain.

To my shame, I had to have researchers develop themes on a unique personality for Norfolk as much as I had to do for Devon. It was only the shires immediately bordering on London that I felt I could handle in my own imagination.

I do remember this café, though. And the longer I sit here, waiting for Neil Hampton to show up, the more snippets of my mentor, Martin Ashen, come back to me. Was I really that anxious to rise above Norwich and to become someone in the art world to have gone so docilely as I did? Was the price worth it?

"Mr. Barkley . . . Philip. I'm sorry I'm late."

I look up and see the young man I met at the art institute earlier in the day. He showed such promise and I told him so. The canvas he was working on exhibited talent and imagination; it just lacked a few strong brushstrokes to bring the perspective into control. And he, he himself. So sultry of looks. Dark curly hair, like an unruly crown, and the violet eyes and the artfully sported brush of a five-O'clock beard, giving his strong facial features exactly the look that my researchers told me would reflect the seafaring folk that settled the Norfolk coast and beat off the invasions of the Danes and merged their DNA with the French aristocrats fleeing here from their revolution.

"It doesn't matter," I answer. "You're here now. Please have a seat. Coffee or something stronger?"

"Coffee is fine."

As he sits, I lean over and place my hand on his thigh. I wish to know immediately what he is willing to do for me.

"Have you thought of my proposition? As I've said, you show promise and are, I think, wasting your talent here in Norwich. I would be happy to mentor you—if you will come to London with me."

"I think I do want that, yes," he answers.

I move my hand higher on this high and more to the inside, placing an index finger on the bulge of his crop.

"You do understand what I am proposing, don't you? For me to be able to work with you, the relationship will have to be total. I must know you fully. You will have to lie under me. And I will sketch you after sex—for my own uses."

"Yes, I understand." He has said that with a clutch in his throat, but I look into his eyes. So young; I had to recheck his age to be sure. But, yes, he has that look of wanting London.

About the Author

Habu is one of the pen names of a former supersonic spy jet pilot, intelligence agent, male model, movie actor, and diplomat. A wild youth in South East Asia was spent enjoying whatever sexual opportunities came his way, and much of his gay male writing is about recalling incidents from those days and inventing ones he'd perhaps have liked to experience. He now leads a very quiet and ordinary happily married family life.

An American, he is a published mainstream novelist and short story writer under another name and in another dimension of his life. He has written or cowritten (with Sabb) over 500 published short stories and nearly 100 published erotica e-books, primarily of gay fiction but also memoir, straight fiction and ménage fiction. His hand and creative writing can be seen in stories and books by habu, sr71plt, Dirk Hessian, Shabbu, and Stephen Kessel—among unrevealed others that might surprise readers. The fictionalized GM memoir *Flying High, Diving Deep* is loosely based on his life experiences. He can be found at the adults only gay male site www.BarbarianSpy.com, which he shares with Sabb and Dirk Hessian.

Our authors always like to receive feedback, and appreciate it when readers post reviews at Goodreads, and other sites.

BarbarianSpy

FOR LITERARY HEAT

Not all books listed below may currently be on release.

BOOKS BY DIRK HESSIAN

Xtreme Erotica

The King's Men
Shores of Tripoli
Prophecy of Noto
Pretender's Fate

General Erotica/Romance

Constantinople
The Beautiful Way
Blue and Gray
Colonel's Treasure
Beginning of Time
Labyrinth

BOOKS BY HABU

Gay Erotica

Memoir Faction

Flying High, Diving Deep

Xtreme Erotica

Second Coming
Vortex: Sacrificed by Curiosity
Dark Angel Sounding

General Erotica

Romance

Gotta Keep Trying
Finding Amnad
Platres Conclave

Other

Beyond the Beaded Curtain
Hard Knocks U
Habu's Christmas Balls
My Neighbour's Spa

Man's Man
Trip Money
Clint Folsom Mysteries Compendium Volume 1
Death to Blonds - Stolen Judgment (Clint Folsom
Mystery)
Clint Folsom Mysteries Compendium Volume 2

Grab Bag 1
Grab Bag 2
Grab Bag 3
The Indian Doctor
Sailorboy
Home to Fire Island
The Sporting Life
Brambleton
Fetish Galore!
Choke Hold
Literary Gay Erotica
Cairo Surrender
The Handyman
Homeward Bound
Journey to Mirage
Menage Erotica
13 Ways for Halloween
Luther
The Indian Prince
BOOKS BY SHABBU
Finding Jason
Dirty Pool
Operation Black Jade
Cigars!
Angel in the Barn
Gayly Complicated
Despoiling David
The Tree of Idleness
I Met a Man
The Interview
Rough Road to Happiness

BOOKS BY SABB
The Legend of Holleystone Grange
Surprise Encounters
She is He
Wrong Man
Loyal to his King
Barbarian Tales - Book One - Traveler's Tales
Barbarian Tales - Book Two - Journeys Begin
Barbarian Tales - Book Three - The Inheritance
Barbarian Tales - Book Four - Road to Persepolis
~